THE CHRISTMAS COOKIE CROOK

TERRY AYRAULT

www.dizzyemupublishing.com

DIZZY EMU PUBLISHING
1714 N McCadden Place, Hollywood, Los Angeles 90028
www.dizzyemupublishing.com

The Christmas Cookie Crook
Terry Ayrault

ISBN: 9798673579312

First published in the United States
in 2020 by Dizzy Emu Publishing

www.dizzyemupublishing.com

"THE CHRISTMAS COOKIE CROOK"

By

Terry Ayrault

741 Westchester
Grosse Pointe Park, MI 48230
(313) 610-5439
terryayrault@gmail.com

EXT. - NIGHTTIME— FRANKINCENSE, A SMALL, FICTIONAL VILLAGE

Frosted streets and brick buildings. Children sleep
peacefully in their beds. The midnight moon lights a room
filled with Christmas decorations.

                              V/O:
                In a snowy white village all covered with frost…

A young boy, Nat, and his twin sister (Maddy), are
sleeping. Nat tosses and turns a bit. He's dreaming.

                              V/O:
                Comes the story of cookies…

PUSH IN/DISSOLVE

Inside Nat's brain. Synapses flash and electrodes spark. In
his dream world, we see a world made of Christmas cookies.

                              V/O:
                That, one Christmas, were lost.

The boy heads downstairs. Everything in the house is made
out of cookies. He heads out into the streets of his
village where fresh baked cookie people are coming out of
gingerbread houses.

                              V/O:
                Stolen away from those who would need 'em
                By a sinister plot, and a man forced to cheat
                'em…

Suddenly, a giant man, who is part chicken, picks up cookie
cars and cookie villagers and shoves them into his mouth.
There is widespread panic. Crumbs fly, cookie people scream
and run away.

                              SNAP ZOOM OUT FROM NAT'S HEAD

Nat wakes with a start. He looks over at his sister, Maddy,
still sleeping. He runs to the window, opens it and looks
up. A strange bird sound echoes in the night.

                              SFX:
                Caw-caw!

A weird shadow casts itself upon the house below.

                                        -CUT

FADE IN:

EXT.IN A LOCKSMITH'S WORKSHOP, 6 YEARS AGO - DAY

A man is toiling on what looks like mechanical wood wings
for humans. There are graphic blueprints all about hinting
that the man is involved in a pretty complex project.

                    ANNCR:
            Tom was a locksmith,
            who tinkered and toiled.
            And forged, and welded,
            and polished and oiled…

TOM BUCKLEBERRY (32) a locksmith who loves to tinker, he's a
sincere, well-meaning, lovable, sentimental and handsome man with
delusions of grandeur. He is a proud father and doting husband
whose string of failures have made him a bit unsure of himself as
he continues to measure, drill and saw in his workshop.

                    ANNCR (CONT'D):
            …His lifelong project,
            to utter perfection.
            And, now it was time
            to test the contraption.

                                        -DISSOLVE

EXT. THE TOP OF A CLIFF OUTSIDE OF TOWN - AFTERNOON

Tom's sitting in a catapult on a snowy mountain, wearing
pilot's goggles and the winged contraption we saw in his
workshop. Some important-looking investors and townsfolk
stand by. Plus, a couple of policemen, a photographer,
Tom's wife and two small children.

                    ANNCR (CONT'D):
            The men from the bank,

were there to take notes.
If Tom could succeed,
he'd get all their votes…

Tom lowers his goggles, does one last check of his gear.

                    ANNCR (CONT'D):
          …And they'd give him the money,
          to fund his invention.
          For taking care of his family,
          was Tom's lifelong intention.

Tom pulls a pocket knife then reaches back to cut the rope
behind him. He looks over at the spectators.

                    TOM:
          Gentlemen. I give you…Uh…Wings for Humans?
          Registered trademark!

                    TOM:
          (To his son) I'll be right back, kids!

One of the banker types, wearing a suit, speaks into the
ear of a police chief who is next to Merry.

                    INVESTOR:
          Chief, if this works, that crazy son of yours'll
          be a millionaire.

                    POLICE CHIEF:
          Not my son. He's my *son-in-law*. And if it doesn't
          work, maybe my daughter will move back in with us
          where she belongs. I call that a "win-win."

CHIEF DAVID WILLIAMSON (mid-60s), bald, mustached, no-nonsense,
tough, naysaying police chief father-in-law of Tom. A curmudgeon
who feels Tom's not good enough for his little girl and
grandkids.

Tom finally cuts through the rope and the catapult launches
him into the air. He flaps his makeshift wings and flies in
place for a moment, as the people in the crowd look amazed,
but Tom falls out of frame quickly.

                    CROWD:
          Ooh.

> TOM:
> Uh-oh.

From the POV of Tom, the ground is getting closer below. He's panicking. He reaches for a pin on his backpack and pulls it. The parachute doesn't open. Tom's twin babies sit wide-eyed in their stroller.

> MERRY:
> Thomas!

MERRY BUCKLEBERRY (30), is the proud, cute and petite wife of Tom. She's a smart, grounded, strong-minded, caring matriarch who always supports and believes in her husband and is devoted to her family. She is mortified as Tom falls to his demise.

Tom lands in a mound of snow below and disappears, leaving his body outline behind.

> TOM:
> (MUFFLED) Ummmpphf. That's gonna leave a mark.

At the top of the cliff, William puts a hand on Merry's shoulder.

> MERRY:
> Thomas?

> POLICE CHIEF:
> I'm so sorry, Merry. He was a brave fellow.
> Truly…a brave fellow.

Merry sadly lowers her head. Her kids in the stroller begin to tear up.

> NAT:
> Daddy?

> -CUT

EXT. THE BOTTOM OF THE CLIFF - SAME AFTERNOON

> TOM:
> Gee willikers!

Tom climbs out of the mound of snow. He looks down,
disappointedly at his broken wooden wings--then back up
toward the top of the mountain.

                         TOM:
              (SINGING)I can't do anything right.
              I try and I try with all of my might.
              But nothing I do
              All day and all night
              Can help me do anything right.
              I can't do anything right.
              Try as I might to reach a new height,

Tom gathers up his wings and parachute. He begins to trudge
through the snow. *Flashback to a young Tom designing a toy
plane out of wooden toy parts. He launches it into the air.
It crashes. He looks disappointed.*

                         TOM:
              I've spent all my life
              studying flight
              But I can't do anything right.

Tom continues to walk. He puts the wooden wings, the
harness and the whole contraption into a pile and sets it
on fire. He looks forlorn watching it all burn.

                         TOM:
              I can't do anything right.
              At the end of the tunnel
              There may be a light
              But, I can't do anything right.

                         (BRIDGE)
              Can't be what I want to be
              It starts and it ends with me
              My family depends on me
              But, I can't do anything right.

Tom pulls out his wallet and looks at a photo of his wife
and kids. A tear falls from his eye and hits the photo. He
wipes it off but he accidentally drops the photo into the
fire. He panics and pulls it out. The fire has singed the
photo and melted the faces of his wife and kids. He puts
the the photo into a pocket, not noticing the small man
standing behind him.

                    TOM:
          It's looking quite odd, you see
          It's always an odyssey
          I think I might be losing my fight…
          'Cause I can't do anything right.

                    JAHOSAPHAT:
          Eh…you alright, sonny?

JAHOSAPHAT B. HIGGINS THE THIR (75), A chubby, white-bearded,
third generation scientist and a multi-millionaire recluse elf
and a master of disguise. He is a sweetheart at first, but behind
his twinkling eyes is something sinister.

Tom flinches as he sees the man standing there.

                    TOM:
          Jiminy Christmas! You scared the
          daylights out of me, Mister.

                    JAHOSAPHAT:
          Oh, well, my apologies, Thomas.

                    TOM:
          Wha? Wait. How did you know my name?

The old man looks at Tom strangely.

                    JAHOSAPHAT:
          Well, it's right there on your flight suit.

Tom looks down to acknowledge his name on his flight suit.

                    TOM:
          Oh… Right. And you are?

The man looks over at the other scraps of Tom's wings that
haven't been used as firewood yet.

                    JAHOSAPHAT:
          Name's Jahosaphat. Jahosaphat B. Higgins the
          Third, to be precise. Pleasure to meet you.

Jahosaphat extends his hand to Tom and the two men shake.

                    TOM:
          Er, likewise.

Tom bows to the old man awkwardly, then begins to walk away
from the small inferno.

                         JAHOSAPHAT:
               Quite a free fall you took there.
               Looks like some contraption.

                         TOM:
               Oh, yes. Those are my "Wings For Humans."
               Registered trademark, patent pending.
               (SARCASTICALLY) My, "ticket to fame and fortune."

Tom makes air quotes with his fingers.

                         JAHOSAPHAT:
               And, how's that working for you, Thomas?

Tom pulls out a mobile phone from a pocket. He looks the
broken device. He tries and fails to turn it on.

                         TOM:
               Not good. (Sarcastically) And it just keeps
               getting better.

He holds the phone up to show Jahosaphat.

                         TOM:
               And now I get to crawl back with my tail between
               my legs and be the laughing stock of
               Frankinsence. Once again.

                         JAHOSAPHAT:
               Well, that doesn't sound very fair.

As the two men walk down the street, Tom picks up some snow
and makes a snow ball.

                         TOM:
               It's not fair to my poor wife and kids…

Tom throws the snowball up in the air and it lands on a
rooftop then slowly begins to roll down the roof.

                         TOM:
               They get to grow up with a loser for a father.

The snowball, now huge, hangs on the edge of the roof.
Then, falls off the roof altogether.

                    JAHOSAPHAT:
          Hm. Well, now Thomas, what if I told
          you that I might be able to help you?

The snowball lands on Tom's head, covering him with snow.

                    TOM:
          Uh…as you can see, I'm pretty helpless, mister.

                    JAHOSAPHAT:
          I don't think so. In fact, while I was watching
          you fall from the sky, I was reminded of all the
          great inventors who have fallen before you.

The two men pass by some ice carvings of DaVinci's
Vetruvian Man then, Galileo on his telescope. Then, Santa
Claus coming down a chimney.

                    JAHOSAPHAT:
          DaVinci. Galileo. Claus. They all had to fail
          before they got back up and got it right.

                    TOM:
          Well, I've certainly done my fair share of…
          wait, Santa Claus was not a failure. C'mon?

Tom brushes some snow off the Santa Claus ice sculpture.

                    JAHOSAPHAT:
          On the contrary, Thomas. Claus was a huge
          failure. He tried everything to get his reindeer
          to fly…built them wings like yours, tried
          attaching rocket engines to the poor things.
          Then, when all his hope was lost, Santa's top elf
          stepped up and helped him develop the real magic
          behind those flying reindeer.

                    TOM:
          What?

                    JAHOSAPHAT:
          Sure. But, has anyone ever heard of Colonel
          Jahosaphat Bartholemew Higgins? No. Because
          as soon as this Claus got his grubby hands on

the secret to the flying reindeer, he took all
the credit. Never once mentioned it was developed
by that top elf. My grandfather! And for that, I
will always know Santa as a great failure.

                    TOM:
Wild. I've never heard that story. So, what's the
magic?

                    JAHOSAPHAT:
Now, slow down, Son. Grandad destroyed the plans
before he passed.

                    TOM:
That's a shame. I'm so sorry.

                    JAHOSAPHAT:
Yes. Well, fueled by my grandfather's dreams, my
father also tried to devise a system that would
help animals to fly on their own. I believe he
nailed it. In fact, NASA bought dad's plans in
the 1950's in an effort to put a monkey on the
moon.

                    TOM:
 A monkey on the moon? That's amazing.

                    JAHOSAPHAT:
Yep, when I was young, I found a copy of Dad's
journals in an attic trunk. I've studied them my
entire life. And now, with my incredible legacy
at my disposal, I too have developed a system
that, I believe, will allow a man, like you, to
fly without the help of a machine.

                    TOM:
    That's…wow…that sounds great.

                    JAHOSAPHAT:
And Thomas, I believe that with my know-how and
your passion, we can make it all a reality. So,
I'm proposing that...wait for it…you come work
with me, right now.

The two men walk past shrubbery cut into strange geometric
shapes that seem a bit dark and evil.

                    TOM:
I'm flattered, Mr. Jahosaphat but…

                    JAHOSAPHAT:
Ah, before you decide, Thomas, consider that
I'm willing to pay…big time. Here is my proposal.

The old man hands Tom an envelope and Tom opens it.

                    TOM:
Wha!...Wha?..Are you kidding me?
This is…this… I've never seen so many zeroes!

Tom begins to pace. He hyperventilates into a paper bag he
has produced from a pocket.

                    JAHOSAPHAT:
Now…there is one teensy catch, Thomas.

The two men are now in front of a cobblestone driveway.

                    TOM:
Catch? What's that?

                    JAHOSAPHAT:
It's an add-on to a deal. Something thrown in for
good measure. A bonus, if you will.

                    TOM:
No, no…I mean, I know what a catch is. What's
your catch?

                    JAHOSAPHAT:
Oh. Well. Yes. You come to work for me…
immediately.
                    TOM:
Uh…okay, you said that. I'll just have to check
in with the wife…I…do you… have a phone… I
could…?

Tom looks down at the broken phone in his hand.

                    JAHOSAPHAT:
No. No. That's the catch, Thomas. When I say
immediately, I mean right this instant. No
checking in. No phone calls. No goodbyes. I want
you to help me for five years straight.

Uninterrupted. Unbothered. Unfriended, un-
familied. Right <u>now</u>.

                    TOM:
But, I have twins…and a wife.

Tom opens his wallet and shows the photo of his wife and
children to Jahosaphat. Jahhosaphat looks at the
burnt/melted photo strangely. He can't see the faces of the
people in it.

                    JAHOSAPHAT:
I know you do. And, based on that fall you
just took, I'm guessing they won't expect you
back soon. In their eyes, I'm afraid you're good
as gone. That's why I also brought you this.

The old man hands Tom another envelope.

                    TOM:
What is?…

                    JAHOSAPHAT:
Call it an insurance policy for you—As I'm *also*
taking a leap… of faith, that is.

                    TOM:
What does that mean?

                    JAHOSAPHAT:
It's a metaphor. It means I'm not super confident
and I'm taking a chance on you.

                    TOM:
No. I know what a leap of faith is. I just need
to know what this means… to *me*.

                    JAHOSAPHAT:
Well, Thomas, that is a statement from a bank
account in Merry's name. For every hour you
spend working for me, I add 50% of your earnings
into that account. Your wife, Nat and Maddy will
be more than taken care of while you're gone.

                    TOM:
Okay. First, how do you know the names of all
my family members? And secondly, did I mention

that this is a lot of money?

            JAHOSAPHAT:
Money is no object when you're out to change the
world, my friend. Now, imagine the faces of your
family members in five years, when you're all
back together and filthy rich?

            TOM:
Wait, you didn't answer my first question.
How do you know my family?

The old man reaches into his coat pocket once more.

            TOM:
Oh, geez, another envelope?!

The old man pulls out his mobile phone.

            JAHOSAPHAT:
What? No. My phone. I know all about you thanks
to a little something I call,"social media."

            TOM:
Wait, you've been stalking me on the Internet?
This just keeps getting creepier and creepier.
And I can't even say goodbye to my family if I
come work with you? (Sarcastically) *Sounds* legit.
You want to sell me some real estate in
The North Pole while you're at it? Heh-heh.

            JAHOSAPHAT:
I'm afraid your family would be too much of a
distraction for our important work, Thomas. So,
yes, it's the conditions of the contract. Look,
I'm a very busy man so, if you want this once-in-
a-lifetime opportunity, I'm afraid you're going
to have to make a decision. Post haste.

            TOM:
            What's that?

            JAHOSAPHAT:
What's the decision? Or, what's post haste?

                    TOM:
          Yeah. See. This time, I don't know what "post
          haste" means.

                    JAHOSAPHAT:
          It means "without pause."

                    TOM:
          Oh, like me? I'm without paws. Heh-heh.

He holds up his hands and shows the old man both sides of
them by turning at the wrists.

                    TOM:
          'Cause I have hands. Right? I'm…

                    JAHOSAPHAT:
          I think your dad jokes are just your way of
          stalling, Thomas.

                    TOM:
          Okay, okay just give me a minute.

                    JAHOSAPHAT:
          You have exactly sixty seconds. And…go.

The old man holds up his phone to Tom to show him that the
stopwatch App is on, counting down from 60 as tense music
plays on his phone. Tom looks over at the old man as if to
say, "really?" The old man shrugs.

                    JAHOSAPHAT:
          It's part of an App I've created. Pretty cool,
          eh?

                    TOM:
          Ugh.

Tom walks away and begins to pace back and forth while
weighing the pros and cons with his hands.

                    TOM:
          This is crazy! This is crazy! This is crazy!
          I can't leave my family. But, then again, they'll
          be so well taken care of. Ugh. This is a huge
          decision, Thomas Buckleberry. But, you'll never

                    have this opportunity again. So, what'ya think?
                    Well, I think you're kinda nuts for talking to
                    yourself. But, this is just too good to pass up,
                    right? And it's for the best for everyone. Oh!
                    Forgive me Merry!

Tom suddenly stops in his tracks. He looks at the old elf.

                              TOM:
                    Alright, alright. Mr. Jahosaphat,
                    I'll take the deal!

The two men shake hands heartily.

                              JAHOSAPHAT:
                    You won't regret it, Thomas. Together, we're
                    gonna fly. Quite literally!

MUSIC TRACK OF "I CAN'T DO ANYTHING RIGHT."

The old man wraps an arm around Tom and they walk off
together bantering.

                                                        -CUT

INT. BELOW CLIFF WHERE TOM LANDED IN SNOW - NEXT MORNING

Chief Williamson and other policemen are investigating the
scene. We can clearly see the imprint of Tom's body in the
pile of snow and an opening where he walked away. While
William looks up toward the top of the cliff, a deputy
approaches him with what looks like a goggles.

DEPUTY COLBY (26), The Police Chief's first mate and loyal
underling is green but has a heart of gold as he cares about his
job and the community. An eager assistant, he's very "by the
book."

                              COLBY:
                    Sir…uh…there's no sign of your son-in-law. But,
                    we did find these.

The deputy holds up Tom's goggles.

                              POLICE CHIEF:
                    (KNOWINGLY) Hm. No other trace of him? You sure?

                    COLBY:
It's like he just disappeared. I mean, maybe he
flew off somewhere after all.

                    POLICE CHIEF:
Uh, you do know you're talking about my
son-in-law, right, Deputy?

The Deputy nods his head. William smirks a bit. He takes a
deep breath.

                    POLICE CHIEF:
Well, the search is over. I'm going to call it
off. Which means I gonna have to pronounce the
missing person… a gone-er.

                    COLBY:
But he could still be out here somewhere, sir.

                    POLICE CHIEF:
No, he's not. He's a goner.

                    COLBY:
But…

                    POLICE CHIEF:
Stand down, Deputy! The search is called off.
Go on home everyone!

                    COLBY:
We can't just…

                    POLICE CHIEF:
You're about *this* close to losing that badge,
Colby! Now, sound the alarm to call it off!

                    COLBY:
(UNWILLINGLY, THROUGH MEGAPHONE) Okay.
Let's pack it up, folks. Nothin' to see here.

The Chief turns his back on Colby and gets a devious smile
on his face.

                                              -CUT

EXT. (THEN INT.)--JAHOSAPHAT'S MANSION ON THE PORCH, THEN
INSIDE THE FRONT DOOR - DUSK

The old man and Tom walk through the front door and into
the foyer where Tom can't believe his eyes.

                         TOM:
              Wait, this is *your* place?

There is a suit of armor in the foyer and a decorative
chandelier hanging from the ceiling. Beautiful wood accents
surround the round foyer with black and white tiled floor.

                      JAHOSAPHAT:
              Well…my father left me the family fortune, of
              course. And I've been rather successful with my,
              uh…shall I say, *investments*.

Behind the front door, eager servants await the master of
the house and his new friend. This strange collage of
people all seem very nice.

                      JAHOSAPHAT:
              Thomas, I'd like you to meet the members of my
              helpful team. Everyone, meet Tom.

                       SERVANTS:
              Hello, Tom! Welcome! Etc.

The old man looks to Ignacious, for immediate assistance.
The others leave the scene.

                      JAHOSAPHAT:
              If you don't mind, Thomas, I have some work to
              do. This is Ignacious…

Tom and the rotund elf shake hands. The houseman elf bows.

IGNACIOUS (40), Jahosaphat's houseman. He, like all the
other house servants, leads a dual life. He is quite sweet
and a bit naïve. With a baby face and skin, he's got an
innocent quality. Also known as The Fruitcake Pusher.)

                      JAHOSAPHAT:
              …He is my houseman. He'll make sure your stay
              here is a pleasant one. Iggy, see to it
              that Mr. Buckleberry gets every comfort he

                    requires, and please bring him to the dining
                    room for supper--precisely at eight.

The old man walks away and slyly looks back over his
shoulder at Tom. Ignacious grabs Tom and begins to escort
him out of the foyer. The old man shouts back.

                         JAHOSAPHAT:
                    Please make yourself at home, Thomas!
                    Mi casa es su casa!

                            TOM:
                    Ope. I know what _that_ means…My house is uh…Sue's
                    house, er, something…like…that.

                         JAHOSAPHAT:
                    I'll see you at eight!

The female servant appears and walks with Tom and the elf.
She takes Tom by the hand and leads him up the stairs.

EDISON (age-unknown) is Jahosaphat's maid with unusually long
arms and sharp features. She is tall and lean and no-nonsense.
She has an Eastern European look and accent as she begins to
sing.

                          EDISON:
                    There's a sense of something special
                    The stars have all aligned
                    It's your chance, it's your story, it's your
                    time.
                    Let's go on this magic journey,
                    Take my hand and we can fly
                    To a place, where your dreams are not denied.

As Tom and the maid walk down the hall, the light changes.
The plants perk up. The color gets more intense. Old
portrait paintings on the wall begin to follow Tom with
their eyes. They join the singing.

                            ALL:
                    Things are looking up,
                    It's easy to believe.
                    Things are looking up,
                    Like everyday is Christmas Eve.
                    You're feeling good
                    And, gosh you know
                    Everywhere you choose to go…

> It's time to live it up.
> 'Cause things are looking up.

They move through the the mansion, making their way into a game room. Everything Tom participates in, he wins. He plays pool with a robot and beats him. Then, he bowls against a different robot and gets a 7/10 split. He dances like a pro under a disco ball, etc.

                    IGNACIOUS:
> Things are looking up,
> The you you knew is new now
> Things are looking up,
> With everything you do now.
> The future's yours
> And you should know
> No matter where you choose to go…
> Don't give in to giving up.
> 'Cause things are looking up.

The elves whisk Tom into a workout room where a personal trainer awaits. He immediately puts Tom on a treadmill and we cut to various shots of Tom's workout, sauna, massage, etc.

                  TRAINER/AZAR:
> Things are looking up.
> I can tell, you look relaxed now
> Things are looking up
> You seem so healthy, not so taxed now.

AZAR, (40-something) is The Candy Cane Klepto. A musclebound health nut and Jahosaphat's personal trainer, Azar has extremely large muscles. He wears a weight belt everywhere. He's also Jahosaphat's head of security. He is second-in-command in Jahosaphat's Anti-Christmas Army.

Tom is now on an antique treadmill. The background scenery changes behind him as he runs. A dangling donut on a string falls from the ceiling in front of Tom and he tries to bite it. The trainer reaches over to turn up the speed. Tom runs super fast. Somehow, he keeps up, still pursuing the donut.

                  TRAINER/AZAR:
> With every step you're taking
> You feel the whole world's for the taking…

Dissolve to Tom who is now on a vibrating belt machine, smiling and laughing as he tries to drink water and sprays it all over his own face.

                    TOM:
         I feel as lively as a pup,
         'Cause things are looking up.

Now showered, Ignacious escorts Tom to a tailor's fitting room in the mansion. The tailor measures Tom for a suit. He must get up on a ladder to measure Tom with measuring tape. The ladder strains. Ignacious, turns his back while the tailor measures Tom's inseam.

MELKY (30), Jahosaphat's short and portly tailor. A former competitive eater, Melky is as lovable as he is role-poly. He's alsoknown as the Egg Nog Napper.

                    MELKY:
         Things are looking up.
         Happy comes in many sizes
         Things are looking up
         And life's full of surprises.

Tom blushes. He is now in his underwear, in a salon, getting a manicure by a salonist. She buffs his nails. He looks at them shining and likes what he sees.

                    SALONIST:
         Every problem seems abolished
         Every issue's brightly polished

Gaspar offers Tom some hot chocolate. Tom gets a mug and gestures for the chef to pour away.

                    GASPAR:
         Allow me to fill your cup.
         Now that things are looking up.

Melky the tailor has sewn together a new smoking jacket for Tom. Tom tries on the red velvet jacket and it fits perfect. Tom puts out a goblet and a waiter fills it with rich hot chocolate. Tom dumps the cocoa over his head like a winning coach. The whole crew of workers surrounds Tom for the crescendo.
                    TOM:
         Whoo! That's hot!

                    ALL:
We don't mean to sound abrupt.
But things are truly…absoluly…
though sometimes, it truly seems unruly…
We're all just warming up.
And things are looking up.

                                        -CUT

INT.   IN FRANKINSENCE FUNERAL HOME- DAYTIME

Merry and the twins are at a funeral. Photos of Tom on an
easels and flowers all around. Merry sadly speaks to guests
as her father, the Police Chief, approaches. He's eating,
nonchalantly, off a plate.

                POLICE CHIEF:
Merry, your mother and I have decided
that you need to move back in with us.

                   MERRY:
                   What?

We see that William has a large piece of lettuce stuck in
his teeth.

                POLICE CHIEF:
We've got plenty of room for you and the twins.
We've got cable…Free wi-fi…It'll be the perfect.

                   MERRY:
Are you serious?

                POLICE CHIEF:
You can have the room at the top of the stairs
and the kids…

                   MERRY:
It's not happening, Dad.

                POLICE CHIEF:
Merry… at some point you're going to have to
accept that he's not coming back.

                    MARGARET:
          Oh, honey, your father just wants what's best
          for you and the children.

MARGARET (62), Merry's petite, docile, unassuming and quiet
mother is very sweet and rational. But, also a bit flighty.
Plus, she wouldn't dare cross her husband.

                    MERRY:
          Are you kidding? How do either of you
          know what's best for us?

                    POLICE CHIEF:
          I'll send for the moving company tomorrow morning
          to get you all packed up.

                    MERRY:
          No…moving co…Are you not listening to me? He may
          be gone, Daddy. But, Tom's always home.
          With us. In *our* home. We're not going anywhere!
          And, you've got a giant piece of lettuce
          stuck in your teeth!

Merry angrily storms away from her father, grabs the kids
in a stroller and slams the door.

                    POLICE CHIEF:
          Oh, come on! Merry! Wait!

                                              -CUT

INT-NIGHT--BACK AT THE MANSION

Ignacious holds a door open for Tom as he walks into a
formal diningroom. The old man is sitting at the end of the
large, full dining room table in a smoking jacket.

                    JAHOSAPHAT:
          Thomas, I hope you enjoyed your day at my quaint
          abode.

Tom looks over the table and the feast in front of him.

                    TOM:
Quaint? This is quaint?

                    JAHOSAPHAT:
Yes, well…we think of this as our opportunity to
sit down, break bread together and talk about the
day's goings on. I'm guessing that you've noticed
something unusual about my staff?

                    TOM:
Oh, yes! They're all so nice.

                    JAHOSAPHAT:
Uh, if you say so. But, you may have also noticed
that they all have quite "unique" shall I say,
"character attributes."

We pan around the room from Tom's POV and see some of the
staff. It dawns on Tom that they have some unusual
deformities that he hadn't noticed before.

                    TOM:
Uh...wow. Now that you mention it…they're
all really amazing singers. It's like they're
a touring company for some off Broadway version
of the Sound of Music. This one?...

Tom acknowledges Ignacious.

                    TOM:
…Voice of an angel!

                    JAHOSAPHAT:
Hm. Interestingly, you have been able to look
beyond their freakish—uh, characteristics—and
have treated my staff as you would treat anyone
else. To that, I say, 'bravo,' Thomas.

                    TOM:
Well, like I said, Jahosaphat, everyone's so nice
I…

                    JAHOSAPHAT:
Mm. You're a very gentle man, Thomas Buckleberry.
Ignacious! Bring us both a mug of egg nog.
We need to toast this gentleman in our midst.

Igancious clumsily leaves the room then, quickly re-enters with a tray. On it are two frosted moosehead glasses of cream-colored egg nog. The two men each take a glass mug and toast.

> JAHOSAPHAT:
> To Thomas Buckleberry. The richest man in Bedford Falls!

> ALL:
> Here! Here! Etc.

> TOM:
> Oh, no. I'm far from rich. And um, I'm from Frankincense. Not Bedford Falls.

> JAHOSAPHAT:
> It was from an old movie, Thomas. One I can't stand, by the way.

> TOM:
> Oh..oh…right. I mean…

Thomas puts his hands to his face like MacCauley Caulkin in Home Alone. He screams.

> TOM:
> Aaaaaah! Right?

Nobody in the room understands or reacts to the reference.

> TOM:
> *Home Alone*? No? Anyone? Wow.

Tom looks around the room for a reaction. He changes the subject then quickly reaches for his cup and takes a drink.

> TOM:
> Ooo. Egg nog. You know, I haven't had egg nog in years. I love egg nog.

> JAHOSAPHAT:
> Is that so?

We see that Tom now has a giant egg nog--miraculously curly-- mustache.

                    TOM:
     Mmm. Yeah. Ya know, come to think of it,
     nobody drinks it anymore.

Jahosaphat looks knowingly at Tom.

                    JAHOSAPHAT:
     It's not that unusual, Thomas…for the
     things we love to disappear.

As Tom begins to ponder about the holiday, his egg nog
mustache has grown into an egg nog goatee.

                    TOM: .
     Ya know, it's weird. In Frankincense, we
     haven't had egg nog in like, forever. We've got
     eggs. We've got milk. But no nog. It seems like
     everything Christmas-y has been disappearing. Egg
     nog…gingerbread. If you want candy canes, you
     have to import them from another county.

As the men speak, a couple of servants bring them platters
filled with food. Jahosaphat gets up from the table and
walks around, towards Tom.

                    JAHOSAPHAT:
     Maybe Frankincensians are becoming more like me
     and just sick of this whole nonsense called
     "Christmas."

Jahosaphat looks out the window.

                    TOM:
     Sick of it? Nah. People love Christmas. They
     can't get enough of it. But, like I said, all the
     really good Christmas stuff just seems to be, I
     dunno, going away.

                    JAHOSAPHAT:
     Well, it's an interesting discussion, but,
     probably best left for another day, Thomas!
     Besides, we're here to talk about your big idea:
     Men being able to fly—under their own power!

                    TOM:
     Well, it's been a dream of mine, really.
     And I believe I'm—well, we're—so close

to making it a reality…

Tom takes anther sip and begins to feel the effects of
something.

                    TOM:
          Gosh… that really is delicious nog.

                    JAHOSAPHAT:
          And Thomas, I think our little operation
          could make all of your flying dreams come true.

Tom takes another sip from his glass of nog. He wipes his
mustache off with his sleeve.

                    TOM:
          Mmm. So good… One ingredient comes from a
          chicken, the other, from a cow. Together? The
          perfect holiday drink...Wait. Did you just say
          operation?

                    JAHOSAPHAT:
          I did, Thomas.

                    TOM:
          So, you mean "operation." As in our *program* or
          process?

The old man sits down in the chair right next to Tom.
From Tom's POV, the old man starts to look blurry.

                    JAHOSAPHAT:
          No, Thomas. I mean operation as in _your_ surgery.

                    TOM:
          Whoa. Surgery? Phew…I feel funny.

                    JAHOSAPHAT:
          That's about right, Thomas. You should by now.

Jahosaphat looks at his watch as Tom looks at his hands. He
puts two fingers up in the air and stares at them. Then,
bends and wiggles them in front of himself.

                    TOM:
          But…ooh, I've got two fingers.

A white screen is lowered behind Jahosaphat and a film
begins on the screen. It's got a dated look—in black and
white. The lights dim. On the screen, we see visions of a
turkey with a helmet on an operating table.

                    JAHOSAPHAT:
          And soon, you will have _two_ wings. You see, my
          idea is a little more complicated than building a
          set of rudimentary wings out of wood. I'm talking
          about merging—or, more accurately—grafting, a set
          of wings from a large bird onto a man's body.

As he speaks, we see a medical diagram (almost a white
board presentation) on the screen behind Jahosaphat. We can
see—visually—that the plan is for the turkey's wings to be
grafted onto the back of a man.

                    JAHOSAPHAT:
          Then, you will be another soldier in my special
          army. A hand-picked rag-tag team of do-badders,
          built to help end Christmas forever! You see, I
          too have a vision for bettering mankind. And it
          starts with destroying Christmas. And the
          senseless ridiculousness of it all.

Tom studies his hand thoroughly, amazed now that he's
lifting four fingers up and down. Jahosaphat's film
continues on the screen.

                    TOM:
          Army? You've got an army? Ooh, I've got four
          fingers.

                    JAHOSAPHAT:
          Yes. You didn't think all these freaks were just
          my house servants, did you? They're a highly-
          trained, skillful Army of thieves recruited for
          the purpose of ending Christmas! Take Ignacious…

Footage of Igancious directing a kitchen of workers as they
make fruitcakes appears on the screen.

                    JAHOSAPHAT:
          He's not just a houseman. He's also the Fruitcake
          Pusher. He makes thousands of fruitcakes each
          year then passes them out to all. I gave him two
          extra sets of arms so he can make two times as

many fruitcakes. But, fruitcakes are like a loaf
of sticky bread with measels. Nobody ever eats
them, they re-gift them. They're so hard to get
rid of so they end up bringing misery to people
every Christmas! I love it!

We pan to Azar then push past his face to see footage on
the screen of him stealing candy canes all over town. Off
of store shelves, off of Christmas trees, pulling large
decorative ones out of ground, taking them from children,
etc.

                    JAHOSAPHAT:
          Then, there's Azar… He was a trainer and
          dietician. I found him at a medical convention…

*Cut to a scene in the film of a younger Azar and
Jahosaphat, meeting in a lobby of a convention hall,
shaking hands. We see them having dinner, hashing out a
plan on a napkin. They laugh, they scheme.*

                    JAHOSAPHAT:
          …He was giving a keynote speech on the dangers of
          candy canes. How they rot teeth, upset stomachs,
          and can be licked into a sharp candy spear that
          can be used to skewer your cousin. I told him my
          plan to end Christmas and he gladly agreed to
          join the cause—he despised candy canes so much. I
          gave him protein shakes and special vitamins to
          make him unbelievably strong. Then, I made him my
          second-in-command to help me cancel candy caning
          forever.

*In the film we see a candy cane factory shut down. A bunch
of people lose their jobs as security ushers them away. We
see a young Azar in the video, walking off the factory
premises with many candy canes hooked around his arms.*

Now, Melky steps forward. He's wearing a tuxedo and a
cummerbund that's stretched over his tummy. On the screen
behind Jahosaphat we see a flashback of Melky—younger now—
stealing egg nog from various households.

                    JAHOSAPHAT:
          Meet Melky, my butler: The Egg Nog Napper.
          As a former competitive eater, this man has
          single-handedly eliminated any trace of egg nog

in Frankincense. I gave him the expandable second
stomach of a cow so he could drink every bottle
and siphon any truck bringing that
disgusting liquid to our store shelves.

*On the screen we see a younger Melky walking into stores
and drinking egg nog right out the containers on shelves.
Then, in various kitchens, pouring carton after carton of
egg nog down his mouth. Cut to him holding up an egg nog
truck near a "Welcome to Frankincense" sign by a highway.
He begins to suck egg nog out of a hose attached to the
truck. His belly grows bigger and bigger as he drinks.*

Tom starts to swoon as Edison, wearing dark sunglasses is
introduced by Jahosaphat.

> JAHOSAPHAT:
> Oh, and say 'hello' to Edison, The Bulb Buster.
> I gave her the arms of an orangutan so that she
> can reach the strings of lights in even the
> highest of trees. She pulls them off the branches
> and breaks a bulb or two. Then, people have to
> figure out which bulb it is. But, it's nearly
> impossible, so they end up throwing away the
> entire string. Ha! So frustrating!

We see a man in a baker's hat and a Lone Ranger mask.

GASPAR (age-unknown) is Jahosaphat's personal chef and The
Gingerbread Crook. He is a fair-skinned redhead with a few
freckles.

*Footage of Gaspar on the screen on a security camera
destroying an entire gingerbread village at a grocery
store.*

> JAHOSAPHAT:
> And Gaspar, my executive chef. AKA, The
> Gingerbread Bandit. This guy despises everything
> gingerbread. His goal is to eliminate all the
> gingerbread stuff we stuff our faces with each
> holiday season. The houses, the gingerbread
> people. He hates everything gingerbread. Why?
> Because of all the teasing and taunting he
> endured as a child. For <u>he</u> is a ginger himself!

Jasper pulls the baker's hat off of Gasper, revealing
bright orange hair underneath. There is a collective gasp

in the room. Then, Siamese twins, attached at the waist, appear in front of Tom.

THE HUMBUG BROTHERS, HARRY AND HERB (20-something), are fraternal twins who were sewn together by Jahosaphat. Attached at the hip, the boys are still not used to being together, so they tend to pull away from each other often. They are goofy and couldn't be more opposite. One wears a mustache, the other is clean shaven.)

We see photos of the both of them up on the screen, then the photos are merged together, creating one.

> JAHOSAPHAT:
> And, of course, The Humbug Brothers. Herb and Harry. Two men, one goal: Create Anti-Christmas Chaos! Experts at utilizing the Internet to raise suspicion about innocent Christmas traditions, for the sake of turning people against the holiday. They're literally attached at the hip—sewed them together myself—to make them doubly efficient at making the holidays doubly unenjoyable.

Cut to Tom who is confused and out of it. The film ends. The house lights come up.

> JAHOSAPHAT:
> But enough about us, Thomas. This is all about you. Imagine…You'll be able to fly without machinery or an external aviation system. Your wings will be part of you! Operated by your brain. Controlled by your body! Once you have your surgery.

Tom pumps his fist, excitedly, then suddenly realizes he's in trouble.

> TOM:
> Yes! …surgery?

> JAHOSAPHAT:
> You're probably feeling the effects of what I slipped into that mug of egg nog already.

> TOM:
> Is this real life?

JAHOSAPHAT:
It _is_ real life. And soon, you will join me and
my army in making sure that Christmas is no
longer part of our lives!

Tom makes a proclamation. Sticks a finger in the air to
make his point.

TOM:
But I love Cliss…Christmas. Jingle bells, jingle
bells, jingle all the way…

Tom begins to sing, he can't control himself.

JAHOSAPHAT:
Ugh! I hate that song! You won't love Christmas
after this. Because I've injected you with
my Black Anti-Christmas serum. A special formula
that makes people lose their memories of
Christmas altogether. In fact, in five out of
five patients who received Jahosaphat's Black
Anti-Christmas serum, loss of memory—especially
Christmas memories—has been common! Patients were
tested against a control group of those receiving
placebo. Jahosaphat's Black Anti-Christmas Serum
has also been proven to cause deep distain of
Columbus Day, Arbor Day and the 4th of July…But,
enough disclaimer. Ignacious!

A disclaimer scrolls below on the screen while Ignacious
walks in with a syringe on a platter. The syringe has
liquid in it that is black. He injects Tom.

JAHOSAPHAT:
You will soon have your wings, Thomas, and then,
you'll be my First Sergeant in charge of
Christmas Cookie Crookery!

TOM:
(SLURRING) You're diabol…diabolib…you're crazy.

JAHOSAPHAT:
And you are going to be working for me, Thomas.
Not for five years, but for the rest of your
life!

                    TOM:
          Whoa. You are one shick puppy, mishter. And
          I'm...sho…tired…

Tom's head falls down into his soup. The old man gets up
from the table and pulls Tom up from his hair. From Tom's
blurry POV, we see some of the other freaks bring a live
turkey into the room. The turkey looks scared as they strap
it down onto a gurney. Jahosahfat pulls off his smoking
jacket, revealing scrubs underneath. Lightening strikes.

                  JAHOSAPHAT:
          Get both patients prepped. I'll scrub in. Ha! Ha!

                                                    -CUT

INT- IN THE BUCKLEBERRY HOUSE - EVENING

Merry is in the kid's room. She tucks in her three-year-
olds and kisses both of them on the forehead. She walks
into the livingroom and begins to turn off the lights.
Moonlight lights a keychain on a key hanger in her kitchen.
She takes the keychain off the key hanger and heads outside
to Tom's workshop/garage. Merry turns on the light and we
see all of her husband's plans for his wings and various
prototypes and drawings all around. Among all the plans are
photos of his family, including shots of Thomas and Merry
together. She begins to reminisce and sing.

                  (SINGING)
          I don't know where you went
          I don't know why you left
          I don't know why you had to disappear.
          I don't know where you are
          So I ask the midnight star
          And pray to god, someday you'll find me here.

Merry walks through the garage, picking up various
artifacts and photos.

                  MERRY:
          Wherever.
          A lifetime full of dreams are lost forever.
          The plans and hopes and schemes we had

Together.
Have come and gone away,
Just like the weather.
Beyond the great beyond, you've gone. Wherever.

We move out of the garage and across the yard, back into the bedroom of the children. *A Time lapse montage shows the happy couple going through their stages of their young lives together. We see them meet in high school as Merry is cheerleading for the award-winning robotics team Tom is on.*

                    MERRY:
    I never.
    Thought that you would leave and go wherever.
    You were something to believe and now,
    Whatever.
    I don't mean to sound naïve
    But this is better
    At least that's what I tell myself: it's better.
    But, it's never.

Now, the couple are inseperable from each other. They're seeing a movie together on a date. She reaches into Thomas' popcorn. We see them at a diner together, sharing a milkshake.

                    MERRY:
    Wherever you've gone
    Wherever you are
    Whenever you think
    Wherever's not far
    Just know, in your heart,
    You'll always be here with me, dear to me,
    near to me…I wish that you were here and not
    Wherever.

In the montage, Tom says goodbye to Merry as he packs his small car and gets ready to drive off to college. They say their goodbyes.

                    MERRY:
    Whenever.
    I think I can't go on, I just remember
    The warmth you brought to me ev'ry
    December.
    My heart had just one option, that's
    Surrender.

34

Merry is at Thomas' graduation. Then, Thomas starts his locksmith business. Tom begins to show interest in flight. He gets his pilot's license. Merry encourages him the entire time.

                    MERRY:
          It's oh-so clever…
          "After" doesn't always follow "happily ever."
          And lines of love aren't easy to just sever.
          Beyond the great beyond, you've gone
          Wherever.

Now, we see the couple going on a picnic together. Thomas pops the question on one knee. Merry tears up and says, "yes."

                    MERRY:
          Wherever.
          A lifetime full of dreams are lost forever.
          The plans and hopes and schemes we had
          Together.
          Have come and gone away,
          Just like the weather.
          Beyond the great beyond, you've gone
          Wherever.

At their wedding, we can tell that Merry's dad isn't too happy with their nuptials. But, the happy couple are off. On their honeymoon, Thomas hang glides with Merry. They both love the experience. We see other aspects of their lives unfold. Childbirth—twins! We see them having romantic moments and funny moments with their kids.

                    MERRY:
          …I wish that you were here and not
          Wherever.

Now, Merry is back in her room. She turns off the light and adjusts her blanket as she lies down to sleep.

                                        —CUT

INT- THE WAR ROOM IN JAHOSAPHAT'S MANSION - EVENING

Jahosaphat appears in front of his "army." They're all in their evil army uniforms/costumes. Jahosaphat is speaking to the the servants from behind a podium with his official seal on the front of it.

                    JAHOSAPHAT:
          Well, the operation was a success. In time, our
          master plan will be put into action. The
          Christmas Cookie Crook will be joining our
          mission to help wipe out Christmas for good!
          The other members of Jahosaphat's army cheer and
          high five/chest bump and fist bump each other in
          a celebratory fashion.

                      ALL:
          Yippee! Yeah! Etc.

                    JAHOSAPHAT:
          Oh, my trusted army of humble servants, the
          madness of holiday shopping, holiday traffic,
          holiday stupidity, will soon be a thing of the
          past. We're one step closer to a world 100%
          Christmas-free!

The army of servants high five, fist bump and chest bump awkwardly.

                    JAHOSAPHAT:
          I mean, c'mon. Christmas?.. Really? It's so
          laaaame. Such a waste of time and money. Am I
          right?
                      ALL:
          Yeah! You're so right! Absolutely! Etc.

Jahosaphat begins to walk among his people while singing.

                    JAHOSAPHAT:
          There's so much wrong with Christmas
          Why's it still around?
          It's worn us out, there is no doubt,
          It's time we shut it down.

Jahosaphat holds up a snow globe and we push inside to see people shopping, getting into fights over scarves and pushing each other in the line to see Santa.

JAHOSAPHAT:
There's so much wrong with Christmas
I'll make it very plain
Christmas time for everyone's
Become an utter pain.

A couple of kids put the final touches on a snowman. A snow
plow comes by in the street and sprays it—and the kids—with
slush and snow. Cut to a woman in the kitchen, she's burnt
a whole tray of cookies, the smoke alarm goes off. Cut to a
man falling off a ladder while putting up Christmas lights.
Cut to a kid opening a present. It's underwear. He puts it
on a pile with a ton of other pairs of underwear.

JAHOSAPHAT:
Snowman-making, cookie baking
Putting up the lights.
Sleighbells, presents, mistletoe, ugh!
It's like a yellow snowball fight.
There's so much wrong with Christmas
It's really got to stop.
Why bring a tree inside the house
When all the needles drop?

A family brings a Christmas tree inside their house. Pine
needles fly everywhere as they pull it through the door.
They're left with a bare tree.

JAHOSAPHAT:
There's so much wrong with Christmas
The whole thing can't be fixed
It had its run, but now it's done,
So, 1956.

A dad tries to take a family Christmas photo in which
everyone is annoyed, not paying attention and dressed in
ugly Christmas dresses and sweaters.

JAHOSAPHAT:
Christmas dresses, kitchen messes
Sweaters that look awful
We pack old socks with presents…

A man opens his stocking to find a gift card to *The Sock
Emporium*.

                    JAHOSAPHAT:
          Aw, that gift card was so thoughtful.
          So thoughtful.So thought, thought, thought, th-
          th-th-th-thou

We see a man filling his cart with Christmas lights. He
races to his house with the car, reaches in the back and
pulls out a net of Christmas lights. He throws it into the
air, it lands on his house, covering it with lights. The
display looks ridiculous. The man proudly admires his work.

                    JAHOSAPHAT:
          There's so much wrong with Christmas
          Forget the celebration.
          We spend so much on Christmas lights
          And call it decoration.

Cut to a Christmas dinner. It looks like a postcard from
1960 with all the lard-laden foods and jell-o from
yesteryear.

                    JAHOSAPHAT:
          There's so much wrong with Christmas
          Don't even get me started
          Cheese logs, egg nog, Christmas ham
          Being over-Christmas-card-ed.

A mailman drags a huge bag filled with mail down the
sidewalk. We see a store with a sign in the window that
keeps changing, lowering the sale price percentage.
We see lines and lines and lines of people at the Post
Office, at the department store, waiting to sit on Santa's
lap, etc.

                    JAHOSAPHAT:
          Christmas mail and retail sales
          And shopping of all kinds
          Lines and lines and lines and lines
          Did I mention all the lines? Oh…
          There's so much wrong with Christmas
          From the fat man to his sack
          I wish it all came with receipt
          So I could take it back.

A department store Santa lightly pushes a kid off his lap.
The kid has obviously pee'd on the Santa. He's mad.

JAHOSAPHAT:
There's so much wrong with Christmas
Don't have to think it over
When we all know, the ho-ho-ho's
Now starting in October.

Mannequins in a store display window wear a mix of
Halloween costumes and Christmas clothes.
Then, we see kids in a school Christmas play on stage as it
goes horribly wrong—scenes drop, etc.

JAHOSAPHAT:
Christmas plays and busy days
Bing Crosby on a loop.

Intercut of "White Christmas" playing over a speaker in a
department store where people are shopping, annoyed.

JAHOSAPHAT:
Time off work, those elves that twerk

Intercut of a JibJab variety on a computer screen

JAHOSAPHAT:
And no one gives a Yuletide whoop.

Pulling out of the Sno Globe, we see Jahosaphat in a
Rockette-like line with the other characters. They kick
their legs in unison. Then, there's a big finish as they're
bunched together and reaching out with their jazz hands.

JAHOSAPHAT:
There's so much wrong with Christmas
I'll make myself succinct
This nonsense we call Christmastime
Should really be extinct!
Together, we can all make sure
That Christmas, every Christmas, will stink!

The room goes quiet as Thomas shuffles into the room,
breaking up the big finish. He is in a hospital gown and
dragging along his IV. He has found the music delightful
and he's humming along to the tune. But, he looks post op
awful. He is wrapped up with bandages and it looks like
he's wearing a backpack of gauze. He applauds.

THOMAS:
That was beautiful! Bravo!

JAHOSAPHAT:
Boys.

Ignacious and Azar come to their senses and grab Thomas by
the arms. They escort him out of the room. He's delirious.

THOMAS:
Seriously, what a number! Hats off to the
choreographer.

A wing pops out of his gauze backpack like an umbrella
going up. Azar stuffs it back in the gauze "backpack."

THOMAS:
Oop. Wardrobe malfunction. Where are we going?

-CUT

8 YEARS LATER

EXT AND INT. THE ENTIRE VILLAGE OF FRANKINCENSE AND BEYOND
AS WE MOVE FROM HOUSE TO HOUSE, WINDOW TO WINDOW - MORNING

On a television show set playing on tv a show host is
making a special kind of Christmas cookie. As her male
sidekick looks on.

COOKING SHOW HOST:
Now, we make these every year and they are a big
hit at the Christmas party. 'Tis the season
people! And today, we're making chocolate drop
cookies!

(COOKING SHOW HOST (40-something), is an enthusiastic
baker who has her own cooking show with a male counterpart
(50), in front of a live studio audience

SIDE KICK:
Mmmm. They smell wonderful. I can't wait.
Can I eat the cookie dough?

COOKING SHOW HOST:
You don't have to. I already...

SIDE KICK:
No. C'mon, lemme lick the spatula.

COOKING SHOW HOST:
Um, there's raw egg in there.

The side-kick reaches over to grab the spatula, much to the host's chagrin. He holds the spatula in his hand, waving it mockingly at the host. Tempting her to grab it away. He takes a big sloppy lick of the cookie dough on the spatula.

COOKING SHOW HOST:
You're gonna regret that.

SIDE KICK:
Aaah…aaah... Mmmm. (CONFIDENTLY) Am I?

COOKING SHOW HOST:
I was going to say, I already have some baked.

The cooking show host pulls a pre-baked tray of cookies from the oven. He shows them to the audience. People ooh and ahh. The side kick looks full of regret.

COOKING SHOW HOST:
You won't be getting any.

SIDE KICK:
But…I…

The show host begins to distribute cookies to her audience and camera men/studio workers as she begins to sing.

COOKING SHOW HOST:
Christmas isn't Christmas 'til the baking.
Until the lovely baking we're partaking.
The cutting and the kneading, so painstaking.

CAMERA MAN:
But so much worth the effort that you're making.

Pull out from the tv to see we're in a kitchen. The tv is
on a counter. A woman pulls some cookies from an oven. She
puts the tray on a counter for the cookies to cool.

                    NEIGHBOR LADY 1:
          Cookies must be baked at Christmas season.
          Cookies from a store? An act of treason.

A man walks in the room and reaches to take a cookie off
the tray and eat it. His wife takes a dish towel off her
shoulder and snaps him with it so he pulls his hand away.

                    NEIGHBOR MAN 1:
          Think of all the stomachs that you're pleasin'

                    NEIGHBOR LADY 1:
          I don't think so.

Swish pan to another house. Inside, a woman, her mother and
her daughters are making cookies. There are ingredients out
on the counters and piles of cookies everywhere.

                    NEIGHBOR LADY 2:
          If not homemade, you'd better have a reason.

We see kids stealing cookies from a cookie jar. They've
piled up boxes and chairs to get to the top shelf where the
cookie jar awaits.

                         KIDS:
          'Cause cookies must be baked at Christmas season.

Quick swish pan to a bakery. Inside, we see a baker and his
staff also making Christmas cookies. As he sings, he grabs
his giant belly and squishes it to make his point.

                       BAKER:
          Cookies just taste better from an oven.
          Believe me, I could eat a couple dozen.

Swish pan to a woman placing a box of homemade cookies on a
neighbor's doorstep, all tied up nicely in a bow.

                    NEIGHBOR LADY 4:
          A gift that's from the heart
          and made with lovin'.

An older woman answers the door and looks thankful for the gesture. She takes the box of cookies from Neighbor Lady 4.

                         OLDER WOMAN:
          I'll eat one, then share them with my cousin.

Another old lady peeks out from behind the first older woman. She smiles and waves. Swish pan to a grocer at the grocery store. Walking down an aisle. He's got a clipboard in his hand, checking off things.

                          GROCER:
          No one likes the cookies that the store makes.
          They never really seem to sell like hot cakes.

Swish pan to a woman at the checkout counter. A customer has their packaged cookies scanned. The woman cashier comments on the package.

                          CHECKER:
          These packaged cookies make for instant
          toothaches.

Swish pan to Santa putting presents under a tree at a house. He looks at a store-bought cookie on a plate, picks it up, studies it and puts it back down.

                          SANTA:
          I'd rather eat a slice of year-old fruitcake.

Swish pan to Mrs. Claus baking in her kitchen with some elves helping her out. She pulls a huge tray of warm cookies out of an oven and the elves go to town, using spatulas to put them on plates.

                        MRS. CLAUS:
          Every one's a little different, like a snowflake.

We cut back to Merry in her kitchen. She pulls a tray of steaming hot cookies from her oven.

                          MERRY:
          There's nothing like the Christmas cookies we
          bake.(TALKING) Okay, Cookies are ready for
          decorating. I've got colored sprinkles, four
          kinds of frosting, candy beads, candy glitter and

every decorating thing-a-ma-bob you can imagine.
Let's get to work!

The camera pulls back and we see so many cookies piled high
all over the kitchen. Cookies galore are everywhere as Nat
and Maddy's eyes widen and they begin to help out.

                                            -CUT

INT. —JAHOSAPHAT'S MANSION—NIGT

In a giant cage, Thomas sits on a perch in his hospital
gown. He's very sad and holds his head down. Jahosaphat
approaches the cage slowly. He's got something in his hand.

                    JAHOSAPHAT:
          Tommy! Special delivery for The Christmas Cookie
          Crook!

Thomas perks up a bit.

                    THOMAS:
          Uh…

                    JAHOSAPHAT:
          That's you, sonny boy. You're The Christmas
          Cookie Crook.

                    THOMAS:
          Oh, I am? That's me?

                    JAHOSAPHAT:
          Of course it's you. Look at your name tag…The
          Christmas Cookie Crook. Right there. That's your
          name, right there on your tag.

Thomas looks down at a "Hello, My Name Is" sticker on the
vest he's wearing. It says, "Christmas Cookie Crook."

                    THOMAS:
          Hm. Oh.

JAHOSAPHAT:
Yes. You're him. That's you. But, you're not just
The Christmas Cookie Crook. You're only man on
the planet capable of flying without any
assistance.

THOMAS:
What?

JAHOSAPHAT:
Yes. Remember? We went over this many times…You
have a set of extraordinary wings—built for
flight!

As he utters those words, Thomas' new wings spread out
fully—but a little unimpressively. Thomas is taken aback.

THOMAS:
Huh?

JAHOSAPHAT:
Yes! You have super powers: A set of powerful,
glorious wings. Fully-feathered! Aerodynamic!
Magnificent!

THOMAS:
I have wings? Oh…I have wings!

JAHOSAPHAT:
You have ability…like no other man on earth. And,
you have an opportunity to change the world with
those wings.

THOMAS:
Eh, I don't get it.

JAHOSAPHAT:
This is what we've been training for. Starting
today, you can use your wings to rid the world of
something that has caused great despair every
December here in Frankincense, and beyond.

THOMAS:
I'm going to use my wings to get people to stop
texting in theatres?

JAHOSAPHAT:
No. Texting?..No. We talked about this. You're
going to use your wings to fly from house to
house and eliminate every Christmas cookie in the
world.

THOMAS:
Eh, what's a Christmas cookie again?

JAHOSAPHAT:
Wow (that Anti-Christmas serum of mine really
works)… Remember? A Christmas cookie is a small
baked piece—or ball—of decorated sweet dough made
especially to bring joy to Christmas.

Jahosaphat hands Thomas a picture of a pile of beautifully
decorated Christmas cookies.

THOMAS:
Oh…And, uh, what's Christmas again?

JAHOSAPHAT:
Oh, my boy, we have so much to re-learn before
tonight. You're like a clean slate everyday.

Thomas still doesn't understand fully what's going on.

THOMAS:
Oh…uh…thank you?

JAHOSAPHAT:
So, let me ask you, my extraordinaire, do you
want to be a hero? Do you want use those wings
for what they were meant?

THOMAS:
It sounds great.

JAHOSAPHAT:
C'mon! You should be more excited than that.
We're about to change the world! Are you in?

THOMAS:
Yes! I'm in.

Jahosaphat reaches out and shakes Thomas' hand heartily.

                    JAHOSAPHAT:
Tonight, the magic begins. Tonight, your heroics
take center stage. Tonight, The Christmas Cookie
Crook flies!

                                        -CUT

INT. AN ELEMENTARY SCHOOL AUDITORIUM — AFTERNOON

Open on a Christmas play on an elementary school stage. A
little boy is dressed royally, in velvet robes and a crown.

                    BOY:
    I am the ghost of Christmas Present!
    Come to show you the true meaning of Christmas.

The boy, Is a classmate of Nat playing the part of the
Ghost of Christmas Present from "A Christmas Carol")
The little boy points to another little boy on stage who is
playing Ebenezer Scrooge, in a night shirt and cap.

                    BOY 2:
    Oh, great spirit! I've already learned so much
    tonight.

Nat is in the audience. He and his sister (sitting beside
him) are 11 now. He has a smirk on his face as he reaches
into his coat pocket, producing a snowball. His sister,
Maddy sits next to him and tries to look over to see what
he's got in his hand.

                    MADDY:
    Oh-no. Is that what I think it is?

MADDY (11), is Nat's twin sister. She is cute and innocent
but an outspoken rule-follower. She is the yin to Nat's
yang. She is sensitive, rational and careful.

                    NAT:
    Shhh…It's just some snow from outside.

                    MADDY:
    (Whispering) Nat, don't even…

                          NAT:
          This is gonna be epic!

The boys and girls in the play begin to sing a song. A
snowball hits the lead actor in the side of the head.

                          BOY 2:
               OW!

The music stops suddenly. Chaos ensues. The boy on the
stage cries as he points at Nat, who is now ducking in his
seat. The spotlight shines on him. A teacher runs out onto
the stage and looks out at Nat. The principal stands, turns
and sees Nat.

                      MRS. TUCKER:
          Nat Buckleberry! Come with me, please!

Mrs. Helen Tucker (55), is Nat and Maddy's elementary
school principal. She is a very nice woman and an old
friend of their mother. She is not strict but Nat has
obviously pushed her buttons.

                        AUDIENCE:
               Oooooh!

                                                    -CUT

INT. THE SCHOOL PRINCIPAL'S OFFICE — SAME AFTERNOON

A door in a school with frosted glass that reads:
Principal's Office. We push through the door to reveal Nat
looking scared in a chair. Across from him at a big oak
desk is the school's principal, Mrs. Tucker.

                      MRS. TUCKER:
          (SINGING) This is not good Nathaniel Buckleberry.
          Your record isn't teetering on nice.
          In fact, it seems you've been so naughty,
          That I feel I have to offer some advice.
          What's hurting you, has made you blue,
          I know it's left its mark.
          But there's a light, and it'll be alright.

If you just stay out of the dark.

                    NAT:
I don't know what you mean.

                    MRS. TUCKER:
I mean…(SINGING)find the bright side, Nat.
Let sunshine be your guide.
It's the right side, Nat.
You've gotta swallow up your pride.
It's true the world is spinning fast
But all bad things must pass
Find your bright side, it's inside of you…

                    NAT:
(RAP)Well my dad had to fly, took a chance, had to try
Said some things, made some wings
and launched himself into the sky.
He was a man on a mission, who was wishin' he could
fly. By himself ... But, Daddy didn't have to die.
He was a thinker—a tinkerer—with thoughts of something
grand, trying to make his family happy, that'd make
him a happy man.
With a plan to, do what the birds do, man,
Dad went out as a flyer. But he was in a frying pan.
'Cause he fell. Like all good men do, he wasn't
belted.
Maybe too close to the sun, I think his wings may have
melted.
Shoot, he had no chute when he tried so hard to fly
Now, I'm growin' up without a dad I'll never know…
I miss the guy.
When I go out to throw a ball, I throw it up against a
wall
When I learned to ride a bike, he wasn't there to
catch my fall
No dad to read to me at bedtime, no dad to say I'm
getting' tall
No dad to play with me, to stay with me, I've had no
dad at all.
Now, the other kids participate in take your dad to
school day
Me? That day is just another "Time to Break a rule
day."
Always looking for attention, Sometimes actin' like a
fool day.
A trouble-makin', teacher-breakin', time-out takin'
school day.
I know right from wrong, but I choose not to be
selective
I act without thinking and I think as an elective

It's my choice to be devious, to prove my disobedience
But check my life previous, it's part of my
ingredients.

                    MRS. TUCKER:
Find the bright side, Nat.
Let sunshine be your guide.
It's the right side, Nat.
You've gotta swallow up your pride.
It's true the world is spinning fast
But all bad things must pass
Find your bright side, it's inside of you…

                    NAT:
See, when dad went skyward, then came crashing to the
ground
His dreams weren't the only dreams that started
falling down.
My mom and my sister and me, we're havin' trouble
being found
And six years later, I've still got no dad around.
My mother? She's the best, but the rest?
Seems something's missin'
She gives me all I need in life: the hugs and all the
kissin'
But she could never be my father so I'll have to keep
wishin'
That I'll find my daddy someday, in fact, I'll make it
my life's mission.
I mean to act up. I don't mean to be a burden.
But inside I've got a fire and a big part of me is
hurtin'.
But, I know why I'm feelin' bad, of that I'm pretty
certain.
I'm ready to grow up.
My past? It's time to close the curtain.

                    MRS. TUCKER:
No one's saying that it's easy,
No one's saying it's a breeze,
No one's telling you that happiness is given.
You don't always have to wear a smile
Or, dance in every aisle
But the bright side inside you
Makes life worth livin' …
And Nat you've got to… go on… livin'

Merry hurriedly walks in the door of the office. She sees
Nat sitting there as the principal stands up.

MERRY:
Nat!.. Mrs. Tucker, I am *so* sorry!

MRS. TUCKER:
Mrs. Buckleberry, I need to talk with you alone
for a moment. Maybe Nat could wait in the hall?

MERRY:
Of course. Nat, stay out there while I speak with
Principal Tucker.

Nat slowly rises out of his seat. He walks out and quietly
shuts the door. The principal shows great concern to Merry.

MRS. TUCKER:
Merry, we've been friends a long time.
So, I'm just going to be honest with you.
Nat has really been acting out. What happened
today seems like a pattern. I witnessed him
destroying another kid's snowman on the
playground yesterday. The day before that, he
painted this not so flattering picture of his art
teacher.

Mrs. Tucker holds up a ridiculous picture of the art
teacher, Mrs. Popadopolis as a hippopotamus.

MRS. TUCKER:
Now, while it might be rather accurate—when you
compare it to the real Mrs. Popadopolis…

She holds a head shot photo of the art teacher next to the
picture Nat drew and the similarities are striking.

MRS. TUCKER:
It's part of a bigger issue. And, this time, I
think tougher discipline may be needed to
reinforce the expectations we have of him at
school.

MERRY:
Oh, Helen. I'm so embarrassed.

MRS. TUCKER:
I know…Look, Nat isn't a bad kid, Merry, I think
he's just got a lot going on in that head of his.

                    He's told me as much. He really misses his
                    father.

The principal reaches across the desk and grabs Merry's
hand.

                              MERRY:
                    I agree. But, what do you suggest?

                              MRS. TUCKER:
                    Well, I'm going to give Nat tomorrow and Monday
                    off—A little tough love. I'm going to tell him
                    that he's being suspended. But, don't worry, it
                    won't go on his permanent record.

                              MERRY:
                    Thank you. Again…I'm so, sorry, Helen.

                              MRS. TUCKER:
                    Merry, we don't know what's in his mind
                    but we need to find out what we can do to
                    help the little guy get through this. Do you know
                    any male figures who can talk to Nat?
                    What about your father?

Merry begins to tear up. Mrs. Tucker puts a box of tissue
in front of her and Merry grabs one.

                              MERRY:
                    Ugh. I don't know if that's such a good idea,
                    Helen.

                              MRS. TUCKER:
                    Well, there is someone else. We have a new school
                    counselor here that he can talk to. An older man.
                    Nat might like him.

                              MERRY:
                    Well. Okay. I guess there's certainly no harm in
                    trying *something*.

She pushes a box of tissues over toward Merry who grabs one
from the box.
                              MRS. TUCKER:
                    Okay. I'll set it up. Now…Let me ask how *you're*
                    doing, Merry?

                    MERRY:
I'm fine. Really.

                    MRS. TUCKER:
Are you?

                    MERRY:
No. I'm not. I miss him, Helen! Everyday. I keep
thinking that he's just going to walk through the
door one day. And everything's going to be back
to normal.

                    MRS. TUCKER:
Oh, honey…of course you miss him. He was your one
and only. It's okay to be strong and courageous,
but it's also okay to feel sad and to miss him.
And, ya know it's not easy to hear, but there's
always a bright side.

Merry blows her nose loudly.

                    MERRY:
Sorry…I know…I just haven't found it yet.

                    MRS. TUCKER:
Oh, you take care of yourself, Merry. And
remember, this whole town cares deeply about you
and your family…we're always here for you…With
love and support.

                    MERRY:
Thank you, Helen.

Merry wipes her eyes and nose, gets up and walks out of the
room and into the waiting area where Nat is sitting—scared.

                    MERRY:
(Sighs then sternly) Uh…Come with me, mister.
You're in for a long weekend!

Nat slowly rises and they walk out of the office together.
He slinks behind his mother out the door.

                                              -CUT

INT- NAT AND MADDY'S BEDROOM—EVENING

The kids have twin beds separated by a table with a lamp on
it. Their room is very sparse and rather small. Merry sits
on Nat's bed, talking to the kids before they go to sleep.

                    MERRY:
         I'm afraid that I have some bad news, Nat…you're
         grounded. That means no phone, no video games
         and, I'm sorry to say but, no Cookie Exchange
         this weekend. Grandma will come and stay with you
         while Maddy and I go.

                    NAT:
Mom!

                    MERRY:
         That's the way it goes, Nat. You made that little
         boy feel terrible today. You ruined the play for
         the whole audience. And now, Mrs. Tucker is
         suspending you from school for a day. That's some
         serious stuff, Nat. And there has to be
         consequences for that kind of behavior. I love
         you, honey, but what you did was not good.

                    NAT:
         I know. I don't know why I did it, Mom.
         I wish I could take it all back. I just…

                    MERRY:
         What is it, Nat. What's bothering you?

                    NAT:
         It's not fair, mom. All my friends…They all have
         their dads. I'm the only one who doesn't. Every
         year, they ask me where he is. What he was like.
         And who he was. What am I suppose to tell 'em,
         mom?

                    MERRY:
         Well, you tell them your dad
         is always with you. In here...

She points to Nat's heart and then, his head.

MERRY:
…and in here. In your heart. And in your head.
He's always with all of us.

NAT:
I know, Mom. But, I also think he's still around…
somewhere. I just get this feeling. And someday…
I'm gonna go to "wherever" and I'm gonna find
Thomas Buckleberry and bring him back home. I
promise I will!

MERRY:
(Forlornly) Okay, Nat. Okay.

Nat makes a bold statement and a bold gesture with his hand
up giving an oath. Merry smiles but knows it's impossible.
Merry reaches over and turns off the light and kisses both
children on their foreheads.

MERRY:
Well, I'm glad you feel bad about your behavior.
You should. Look, you can help Maddy and I do the
Christmas cookie baking tomorrow morning. But,
like I said, no exchange for you.

MADDY:
It'll be okay, Nat. I'll bring some cookies back
for you.

NAT:
(SNIFFLING) Thanks, Maddy.

MADDY:
It's what big sisters do.

NAT:
You're only seventeen minutes older than me!

MERRY:
Oh gosh, we have so much to do and there's only a
week before Christmas! Goodnight now, go to sleep
you two.

BOTH KIDS:
Goodnight, Mom.

Merry turns the light and a bird-like shadow flies by, casting a shadow on the room. Merry doesn't notice. From outside the window, we see the figure fly off. Merry walks out of the kids room, shuts their bedroom door and becomes very melancholy. She looks up and sees a full family picture on a table nearby. She smiles and sighs.

-CUT

INT.—NIGHT TIME—JAHOSAPHAT'S MANSION

Jahosaphat writes on a whiteboard while conducting a briefing in a briefing room in front of all the other servants in his "army."

> JAHOSAPHAT:
> Ladies and gentlemen, it's time we moved into phase 4 of Operation Finish Christmas Once and For All. Or, eh, OFCOAFA. So far, we've managed to eliminate all traces of egg nog and gingerbread in the tri-county area, wipe out candy canes, ruin millions of Christmas lights and distribute fruit cakes to many. But, it's not enough. So, tonight, this enormous oversight ends for good!

The Old Man pounds the podium he stands at to drive home his point.

> JAHOSAPHAT:
> For six years, this next young man has been in training. He's worked so hard to be the dark, sinister thief he has become (I'm so proud of him). I've stripped him of his moral compass. I taught him how to sneak and how to scheme, how to rob without conscious! Six years of training and now, he is a lean, mean, part man, part turkey—a murky—or, whatever…Ladies and gentlemen, it is without further adieu, and with great honor, that I introduce to you…

An ominous figure appears in the shadows of the room.

                    JAHOSAPHAT:
              …The Christmas Cookie Crook!

Tom spreads his new wings, then, steps out of the shadows
and he is no longer ominous, but looks a bit silly, as he
has turkey wings and is wearing lederhosen with suspenders.
The rest of the army applauds loudly at first then--we can
tell by their disappointment--they consider Tom to look
less than intimidating.

                       ALL:
              Yea...Er…yippee…okay…adequate…etc.

                                              -CUT

EXT.—NIGHTIME—ALL AROUND THE SKIES IN FRANKINCENSE.

Various shots of Tom (now The Cookie Crook) gliding through
the sky. He holds a sack of cookies in his teeth.

                     NARRATOR:
              One man's dreams came true,
              Tom could finally fly
              As he flapped his new wings
              And took to the sky.

Tom comes in for a landing on a balcony. He reaches into
his pocket and uses a skeleton key to open a door. He walks
into the house.

                       V/O:
              House after house,
              He was a man on a mission…

Tom speeds through the house and, suddenly, he's in the
kitchen of the home, opening cookie jars and pouring the
contents into his sack.

                       V/O:
              To steal Christmas cookies…
              He'd raid every kitchen.
              He enters each house
              With a skeleton key.

He de-cookies each home,
And he does so with glee.

The Crook walks out the door and takes off from the
balcony. Off to the next rooftop or balcony entryway.
We see him land in front of a bakery. He uses his key and
walks right through the door. Then, begins to fill his sack
with even more cookies. The sack grows huge.

                                                -CUT

INT. -NAT'S BEDROOM—MIDDLE OF THE NIGHT

Nat gets up out of his bed to investigate a sound
downstairs. He slips on his slippers and robe then tiptoes
out of his bedroom. As he slowly walks down a stairway, he
see's a faint light in the kitchen. He peers around a
corner and sees the Cookie Crook rummaging through a
cupboard. He finds cookies—and empties a jar of them into
his sack. Nat begins to sing.

                    NAT:
          Hey,you,stop that snitchin'
          How'd you get inside this kitchen?
          Why's your nose inside that cookie jar?

At this point, the Cookie Crook has gotten a jar of cookies
stuck on his nose. He shakes his head to get it off, but
the jar is not going anywhere.

                    NAT:
          Hey, you, you're so darin'
          All those cookies that you're snarin'
          Your snitching, snatching ways are so bizzare.

He gets the jar off, then plops a cookie into his mouth.
Chewing it quickly without tasting it.

                    NAT:
          You've got feathers,lederhosen,
          But I don't like the path you've chosen,
          You're a prowler, you're a taker, you're a sneak
          You're horrific and neglecting
          The terrific fun that you're affecting

Stealing cookies makes you nothing but a thief.

Take our treats and take our merry
Take our gravy and cranberry
Take our Christmas, take our Yule
And take our glee

But Christmas without cookies
Is like Star Wars without Wookies
And like Christmas without stockings or a tree.

Hey, you, whatcha seizing?
What you're doing isn't pleasing
Why're you dumpin' cookies in that sack?
Hey you, what're you gaining?
Why is this so entertaining?
To steal something from another
Without intent to give it back?

Take our treats and take our merry
Take our gravy and cranberry
Take our Christmas, take our Yule
And take our glee

But Christmas without cookies
Is like Star Wars without Wookies
And like Christmas without stockings or a tree.

Nat turns on a light.

                    NAT:
          A-ha! What's going on here?

The Cookie Crook is startled. He nervously drops his sack
on the ground and cookies fall out. Nat walks out of a
shadow and into a light beaming through a window, showing
himself to the Cookie Crook.

                    NAT:
          Are you taking our Christmas cookies?

                    CROOK:
          Um…no?

The Cookie Crook uses his foot to hide the sack of cookies
behind him by sliding it across the floor.

                    NAT:
Oh yeah? Then whatcha got in the sack?

                    CROOK:
(Nervously) This? Uh, this is my uh…
a bag full of uh, coal? Yeah. That's right. I
deliver coal to children who've been naughty so
Santa doesn't have to be the bad guy.

                    NAT:
You're kind of embarrassing yourself.

                    CROOK:
Am I? Because I would argue that you're still
asleep, and that this is all an elaborate dream.

                    NAT:
A dream?

                    CROOK:
Of course! I'm nothing but a figment of
your imagination. I'm your mind messing with you.

We can tell Nat's starting to question the scene.

                    NAT:
I guess that…sorta makes sense.

                    CROOK:
Of course it does. What else could make sense?
I mean, why would someone dressed like a
Christmas turkey, swipe Christmas cookies from
someone's cookie jar? It just doesn't add up.

                    NAT:
It's definitely weird.

                    CROOK:
It's weirder than weird. What would someone do
with all those cookies anyway? Right? I mean, is
there like a giant cookie-eating dragon that
needs feeding somewhere? Ha! It doesn't make a
lick of sense.

NAT scratches his head, confused.

                    NAT:
Geez. I must have some imagination.

                    CROOK:
Or maybe you just drank too much hot chocolate
before bed and the sugar's gone to your head.
So, here's what I'd recommend: you tiptoe
back to beddy-bye and don't give this
little scene a second thought. Just lie down,
pull the covers up, maybe fluff your pillow
a bit, and then get back to Z-town.

Nat looks like he agrees. He turns to walk away.

                    NAT:
That sounds like a plan Mister, uh, Cookie Guy.
Wait a minute. I didn't have any hot chocolate.
I…
                    CROOK:
Doesn't matter. You're young, you need your
beauty rest, big day tomorrow…blah, blah, blah.

                    NAT:
Yeah. You're probably right. Uh…thanks?

                    CROOK:
No problemo. Goodnight, Squirt.

                    NAT:
Uh…Goodnight?

As Nat begins to walk up the stairs, the Crook gets ready
to fly out an open window. But, suddenly, something catches
his eye. On a table by the window is a photograph of Merry
and the kids. He stops dead in his tracks.
                    CROOK:
Ah, you know, before you go…can I ask you a quick
question?

                    NAT:
Yeah?

                    CROOK:
Um, who…in the photo on the table. Who is that?

                    NAT:
Oh, you mean the lady? That's my mom.

The Cookie Crook seems intrigued.

                    CROOK:
          Your mom…Hm.

                    NAT:
          Hm. What?

The Crook shakes his head a little to get the fuzz out of
his brain. He can't fully understand what's going on.

                    CROOK:
          Well, I just feel like I know her from somewhere.
          What's her name?

                    NAT:
          Um, it's Merry.

                    CROOK:
          Merry. Hm. Merry...So…familiar.

                    NAT:
          Well…It's my mom, so if this is my dream, it
          makes sense that she'd seem familiar.

                    CROOK:
          You know what my boy, you are one smart cookie.
          Alright then, off you go. Back to bed!

The Cookie Crook flies out of the open window. Nat goes
back into bed, still a bit freaked. He fluffs his pillow,
pulling up his covers.

                    NAT:
          (TO HIMSELF) Whoo. A winged turkey man in
          lederhosen stealing Christmas Cookies? You've
          gotta get a grip, Nat Buckleberry. Sheesh. So
          ridiculous.

                                             -CUT

EXT. --ON THE ROOF OF MERRY'S HOUSE IN THE MIDDLE OF A
MOONLIT NIGHT.

The Christmas Cookie Crook, sits with his sack full of
cookies on the pitched slate roof. He sighs and opens the
bag. Atop all of the cookies is the framed photo of Merry
with her children. He stole it too. He seems very puzzled
as he looks closely at the photo and begins to sing.

                    TOM:
          I know I know your face
          The place to where it takes me
          I know I know your name
          Somehow it still escapes me

Tom imagines memories in his head. We see him with other
people but we cannot make out their faces. They are fuzzed
out and pixilated.

                    TOM:
          I feel as though we shared a life sometime before
          When everything was right, another time before…
          The memories are just so paper thin
          I long to feel those feelings once again…

          It's been too long since I saw you.
          It's been too long since we danced
          It's been too long since you said so long to me.
          It's been too long since I kissed you
          Underneath the mistletoe but somehow you're still
          a perfect memory

          Be my Merry
          Be my Merry

Cut to Merry in her bedroom, unable to sleep. She's lying in bed
thinking about her husband while looking at their wedding photo
on the table next to her bed. As the couple sing their parts, we
cut back and forth between them.

                    MERRY:
          You shimmer when you're here,
          You make my spirits brighter
          The whole world disappears
          Your laughter takes me higher.
          Don't wanna say goodbye,
          When I've just said hello.
          Your arms hold me so tight

             But, I'm scared to let you go.

                      TOM:
          The memories are just so paper thin
          I long to feel those feelings once again...

When we cut to Tom, we see him having a very vague flashback of
Merry and a couple of babies (twins) being born but we can tell
that they are just flashes. Very quick.

                     BOTH:
          It's been too long since I saw you.
          It's been too long since we danced
          It's been too long since you said so long to me.
          It's been too long since I kissed you
          Underneath the mistletoe, but somehow you're
          still a perfect memory
          Be my Merry
          Be my Merry

Tom moves on the roof so that his back is against a dormer.
Merry, meanwhile, is inside, with her back to the wall in
her bedroom. Despite a wall, they are back to back.

                     MERRY:
          I know they say the past is in the past,
          But I'd do anything to get it back.

He inserts the photo back into his sack. He flies away.

                                                  -CUT

INT—POLICE CHIEF'S KITCHEN--IN THE MIDDLE OF THE NIGHT

Police Chief Williamson, in his police-issued pajamas, is
making himself a sandwich. Meanwhile, The Cookie Crook,
holding a bag of stolen cookies, is nervously clinging to
the ceiling above William. One sole cookie crumb falls from
a hole in the bag onto William's sandwich just before he
puts the top slice of bread on it. William senses something
momentarily, then takes a bite of the sandwich. He finds it
delicious. He looks out the window because he feels the

presence but can't see what's outside. We hear William's
wife call him from another room.

                    MARGARET VO:
        Honey? Are you downstairs?

                    POLICE CHIEF:
        I couldn't sleep. Be right up!

                    MARGARET VO:
        Okay. Hope you're not eating!

                    POLICE CHIEF:
        (MOCKINGLY, NONSENSICAL, UNDER HIS BREATH) Humph
        yer not maw maw.

We see the silhouette of the Christmas Cookie Crook fly by
the window going the other way now. William turns to look.
Scratches his bald head. He dumps the rest of the sandwich
in the sink and heads back to bed.

                                            -CUT

INT.VARIOUS LOCATIONS AROUND FRANKINCENSE - EARLY MORNING

We see children all over Frankincense waking up and
excitedly running downstairs to help with the cookies.
Moms and kids are in kitchens, discovering their cookies
have been stolen. Maddy opens a Christmas cookie jar on the
counter and starts to scrounge around in there.

                    MADDY:
        Uh, Mom, there's nothing in the cookie jar!

Merry walks over to the cupboard to look as Maddy steps
aside.
                    MERRY:
        Oh, look in the container on the counter.

                    MADDY:
        Nothing in there either.

                         MERRY:
          Wait, we made six dozen cookies. Where could
          they?…

Merry begins to panic a little. She's really scrounging
through the cupboards. Pulling all kinds of items out of
the oven, the fridge, she's tearing apart the kitchen.

                         MERRY:
          We have no cookies? Nat? Nat!?

Nat comes bounding down the stairs in his pajamas, rubbing
his eyes. He stops at the bottom of the stairs. He's
shocked as reality hits.

                         MERRY:
          Nat? What happened to all the cookies we made?

                         NAT:
          (TO HIMSELF) It wasn't a dream.

The phone rings. Merry answers it.

                         MERRY:
          Hello?...oh gosh, Kathryn?

We split screen to show the woman she is on the phone with—
another mom in the kitchen, obviously in the middle of
baking.

                         KATHRYN:
          Hi, Merry, it's Kathryn from next door.
          Funniest thing. I spent yesterday making cookies
          for Christmas…wake up this morning and they're
          gone. All of 'em. It's like "what the fruit?"

Kathryn Fox (50), is Merry's preppy, wealthy next door
neighbor and a good friend. She is very sensible, honest
and straightforward with a dry sense of humor.

                         MERRY:
          That's so odd, Kathryn. Ours are gone too. I
          don't get it. Where did you have yours?

                         KATHRYN:
          They were all in my Goochy-Goo designer cookie
          jar on the counter…Let me look again…

Kathryn scrounges through a bedazzled cookie jar, finding nothing. Then, she opens a drawer in the kitchen.

                    KATHRYN:
          Let me see… Melon baller. My old mix tape—that's too hot to handle—you know what? No cookies! Yep, they're all gone. I've been cleaned out!

                    SFX:
          Beep.

                    MERRY:
          Hold on, Kathryn, that's the other line.

Another woman is buzzing through to Merry. Now there are three women in three frames on the screen.

                    MERRY:
          Hello?

                    LOUISE:
          Hello, Merry. It's Louise. I've been raided. By cookie pirates, or something. They took 'em all! They took 'em all! Even the ones I made for the cats. They took 'em all!

Louise Bear (40-ish), is another good friend of Merry. She's a nervous Nelly with the weight of the world on her shoulders and she's a bit awkward and afraid. A recluse and a cat lady, we see many cats in around her whenever we see her. Even her clothes are littered with kitty motif.

                    MERRY:
          Louise, I know. Mine are gone too.
          And Kathryn's on the other line saying the same…

                    SFX:
          BEEP.

                    MERRY:
          Hold on, Louise. Someone's beeping through…Hello?

A fourth woman joins the party line and appears as a fourth frame.

                              EMILY:
          Merry? It's Emily. They took my cookies! All my
          beautiful cookies. My chocolate drops, my nutty
          buddies, my gingerbread men, my frosty delights!
          All of them! Ka-put! Gone! Lo, what is a girl to
          do?

Emily puts the back of her hand to her forehead as if she's
going to faint.

Emily Wolf (30-ish) a drama queen and another friend of
Merry's. She is theatrical beyond belief. While she is
always on, she means well and is truly sincere. She always
seems to be in need of attention.

                              MERRY:
          Eh, hold on, Emily.

                              EMILY:
          Don't you hang up on me, Merry Bucklebe...

                              SFX:
                              BEEP

Merry hits the button on the phone again, another call is
coming through.

                              MERRY:
          Hello?

Screen splits again to see another woman on the line.
The woman is obviously stressed and crying.

                              ELLENORE:
          Merry? The Cookies…they're gone! They're all
          gone! (CRYING)

Ellenore Badger (30-something), is Merry's hysterical
friend. She is overly sensitive and tends to cry at the
drop of a hat. Ellenore has trouble controlling her
waterworks whether she's happy or sad)

                              MERRY:
          Ellenore, you've got to calm down. Let's take a
          deep breath. There's got to be a logical
          explanation for this. And…eh…hold on, one second.

ELLENORE:
(Hysterically) I just can't be…be…believe…

Meanwhile, Nat looks down and sees that there is a trail of cookie crumbs leading out the kitchen window. It continues outside and onto the snow on the ground—a cookie crum path that leads off into the distance. He looks at the path and then up to his mother. On the screen, we see that now, all the women in the split screen are visibly upset.

SFX:
BEEP OF PHONE LINE.

Merry answers the other line as the frame is now crowded.

MERRY:
Eh, hold on, Ellenore…Hello?

It's Merry's father, calling from the police station. All the cops around him are upset. They're added as a fifth frame on the screen.

POLICE CHIEF:
Merry…it's your father.

MERRY:
Daddy? The Christmas Cookies...
They've all just…vanished!

We push in on the police chief's face.

POLICE CHIEF:
I know. The folks here are really bent.

MERRY:
I think there's been a caper, daddy.
Every cookie in Francincense is gone!

POLICE CHIEF:
That's ridiculous. Who would steal Christmas cookies?

A deputy walks into the Chief's office.

                    COLBY:
Chief, just got off the phone with Jimmy the
Baker. All his cookies are gone too.

                 POLICE CHIEF:
This is crazy!

A female deputy puts a phone down nearby.

                   DEPUTY 2:
Chief, That was Mr. McCarthy from the grocery
store. All the Christmas Cookies have been
looted.

                    COLBY:
Ya know, my wife went to decorate her
cookies this morning. Nothing in the cookie jar.
And the cookie exchange is tomorrow.

                 POLICE CHIEF:
Diabolical! (To the phone) Merry, we're gonna
look into this. It sounds like a serial culprit.
Someone with no conscience.

                    MERRY:
You probably mean a cookie culprit, Daddy. He
didn't steal any cereal.

                 POLICE CHIEF:
Uh. That's right. A cookie culprit with
absolutely no regard for Christmas spirit.

                    MERRY:
What are we going to do?

                 POLICE CHIEF:
I'm no cookie-maker, Merry, but I'd say you're
gonna have to bear down and start re-baking
everything. We all are.

                    MERRY:
Easy for you to say, daddy. You've never baked a
cookie in your life.

                 POLICE CHIEF:
We'll sure. (Sarcastically) I know it's not as
easy as keeping the streets of Frankincense safe

and sound for all our citizens, but I'm sure
cookie-baking is an integral part of keeping the
peace…

MERRY:

Ugh…

POLICE CHIEF:
Look, I'm sending a deputy over to dust for
crumbs. We'll get to the bottom of this.
Hopefully in time for the cookie exchange.

MERRY:
Oh. I hope so, Daddy. Thank you.

POLICE CHIEF:
No thanks necessary, Merry. This is a matter of
public safety and Christmas spirit. The
Frankincense Police Department was built to
secure both. It's our duty to…

Merry hangs up on her father and get backs to all her
girlfriends talking at the same time.

-CUT

INT. JAHOSAPHAT'S MANSION - EARLY MORNING

Jahosaphat's team has assembled after a night of debauchery
and thievery. The Cookie Crook is still in a foggy daze and
in full costume. Next to him is a giant sack.

JAHOSAPHAT:
So, Cookie Crook, it looks as if you've had a
very prosperous caper. Go ahead and put the sack
on the scale, boys… Yes. That's right.

The Humbug Brothers excitedly pick up the sack and struggle
to do so as neither brother wants to be shown up by the
other. They painstakingly pull off the tie around the sack
and empty the contents into a giant chrome bowl. Millions
of colorful cookies fill the bowl. The scale cannot handle
all the cookies. They overflow. The scale is completely

tipped past its largest amount. Until it reads: "crazy amount." The others in the room are amazed.

                    ALL:
          Ooh. This guy's good, etc.

                    JAHOSAPHAT:
          That's a crazy amount of cookies, son. Why, it
          looks like you may have stolen every cookie in
          Frankincense, m'boy!

                    TOM:
          Uh…lemme see…

 Tom counts on his fingers on both hands, adding things up.

                    TOM:
          Yeah. I'm pretty sure I did.

                    JAHOSAPHAT:
          You…impossible. In one week? How could you…?

                    TOM:
          Well, I *can* fly.

We see security camera footage of Tom landing on porches
all over town, picking locks with his skeleton keys,
walking into houses, storming into kitchens opening
cupboards and stealing cookies—emptying them into his sack.

                    TOM V/O:
          Plus, I made a skeleton key for every lock in
          town so, I get in, get out. Nobody ever knows I'm
          there. Not even a mouse.

Cut back to the other thieves looking impressed and a
little embarrassed by their own pithy piles of stolen goods
near them.

                    JAHOSAPHAT:
          Very impressive. You others could certainly learn
          from "The Christmas Cookie Crook!" Ha-ha!

We pan the other culprits to see there is dissension in the
ranks. Jahosaphat shakes Tom's wing and holds it over his
head like a boxer who has just won a fight. The other
criminals cringe and titter with each other.

                    JAHOSAPHAT:
But, our work is not done, people! We can't stop
now, friends! We must make this Christmas the
absolute worst so that next year, nobody will
want to go through it again!

Ignacious pulls out a pile of envelopes from a safe nearby.
He hands them to Jahosaphat as the old man pontificates.

                    JAHOSAPHAT:
I have assignments for all of you.
Some top secret, dark and loathesome
stuff that's really going to take our operation
to the next level. So, who is going to step up
and really impress me? We're about to find out.
Because tonight, we put the finishing touches on
our plan to ruin Christmas! It's gonna be great!

                                              -CUT

INT-FRANKINCENSE SCHOOL GYMNASIUM--THE NEXT DAY

The whole town is scuttling into the cookie exchange.
People enter carrying trays and trays but without any
cookies. There's a somber mood among the crowd. Women and
children whimper, cry and weep as the talk of the event is
the missing Christmas cookies. Merry walks to a busy table
where other families are seated and standing. She sees her
friends from the phone call earlier: Kathryn, Louise, Emily
and Ellenore.

                    MERRY:
          This is going to be a challenge. I spoke to
          Deputy Colby earlier, the whole area's been wiped
          clean of Christmas cookies.

                    KATHRYN:
We've never had a Christmas without cookies!

                    LOUISE:
David's soccer coach's wife's sister told me this

is the work of a ring of bandits that've been casing our homes for months. Could you imagine?

Emily makes a big theatrical statement. Then, bows when she finishes making it.

                    EMILY:
It's not a random act! And…scene.

                    ELLENORE:
My sister-in-law's brother's great aunt's hairdresser said it was a sign that the world was coming to an end! Oh!

                    LOUISE:
My maw-maw's veteranarian's receptionist said it was cat burglars. Oh, those poor cats, to have a type of burglar named after them.

                    MERRY:
Girls, we have to remember that these are cookies we're talking about. Just…cookies.

                    EMILY:
It's not about the cookies themselves, Merry. It's about this.

Emily puts her arms out and acknowledges the cookie exchange.

                    EMILY:
Whoever did this, didn't just ruin our cookie exchange. They ruined our lives!

From Merry's POV, we look around the cookie exchange at all the desperate faces and glum people.

                    MERRY:
No. You're wrong. Our lives will go on. We can get through Christmas without cookies.

                    EMILY:
We have nothing left to leave for Santa? The poor man's gonna starve! To whom do we look for help? Where do we turn? What do…uh…line?

LOUISE:
What do we do?

EMILY:
Thank you, love: What do we do?

MERRY:
You guys, this isn't the end of the cookie
exchange. We're gonna continue to do this every
year. Whether it's a cookie exchange, a pie
exchange, heck, even a pickle exchange. It's not
about what we're exchanging. It's about what
we're sharing: Stories. Laughter. Good times
together. This is what the cookie exchange is all
about. Us being together… Not the cookies.

KATHRYN:
These cookies may be a little thing. But, they
represent something far bigger, Merry. It's just
another small bite taken out of Christmas. And if
this continues, Christmas is gonna end up
completely wiped out altogether.

ELLENORE:
What are you saying?

KATHRYN:
I'm saying…

Kathryn begins to sing and, as she does, we push into the
fire behind her. Then, in what seems like a continuous pull
back from the fire, the rest of the story (in lyrics)
unfold We almost pass by each of the lines of lyric
happening as they're mentioned. We see the log crackling,
pull back to see the fire, pull back further to see a kid
laughing as he opens a present, etc.

KATHRYN
The crackle the log makes inside the fireplace
The laugh of a child and the joy in their eyes.
The smell of the fir tree the lights look so
pret-ty
The frost on the windows and hot apple pie.

All the women join Kathryn in song. They suddenly sing in
harmony like the perfect Christmas choir.

                        WOMEN:
          It's the little things that
          Truly make up Christmas
          The tiny things
          Like cocoa when it's hot
          The little things
          Put meaning into Christmas.
          And Christmas Cookies really
          Mean a lot.

Now, we're outside the house, we see a telephone line
carrying a voice. We keep pulling back. Now, it starts to
slowly snow large flakes. They fall in slow motion.

                        KATHRYN:
          A long distance phone call, a slow motion snow
          fall
          A seat in a sleigh ride with someone you love.

We follow falling snow onto a sleigh to see a couple on a
romantic sleigh ride together. They pass a nativity scene
in front of a small chapel. We lock in on a star over the
scene.

                        KATHRYN:
          The smile of a stranger, a babe in a manger
          A Northernly star in the sky up above.

The four women appear in front of the manger scene and
continue to sing together.

                        WOMEN:
          It's the little things that
          Truly make up Christmas
          The pretty things
          Like bows tied in a knot.
          The little things
          Put meaning into Christmas.
          And Christmas Cookies really
          Mean a lot.

The women are now in a beautifully decorated room in a warm
home. Around them is an entire family celebrating the
holiday together. A high school kid opens a box of
underwear and socks. But, he doesn't look disappointed.

KATHRYN:
It's the tiniest boxes it's undies and sockses
And grandma's delight when you open her gifts.
The smile on your brother and the one on your
mother
And being together and the spirits it lifts.

All the women sing together. Now back at the gynasium.

WOMEN:
It's the little things that truly make up
Christmas
The small things like excited little tots.

They throw out their hands for Merry to bring up the big
finish.

MERRY:
The little things put meaning into Christmas.
Oh…
And Christmas Cookies really mean a lot!

The women all come together and each takes a bite out of a
very disgusting looking donut.

EMILY:
Ooh. Not the same.

LOUISE:
Inedible.

ELLENORE:
Gross!

MERRY:
Blah!

KATHRYN:
And, those are dog treats.

The women are disgusted, try to use napkins and their hands
to get the taste out of their mouths.

KATHRYN:
Um. They were for Fi-Fi.

She opens a purse and a small snobby dog pops out and
snarls at the women.

                    KATHRYN:
        Sorry.

William walks into the gymnasium and up a stage where a
podium awaits. The Mayor of Frankincense (60-ish), is with
him. The Mayor is a bit bumbling but charming. He's sort of
portly with a bad toupee. He tests the mic by tapping it.
Everyone gives the Mayor their attention. He begins to
speak.

                    MAYOR:
        Test…1..2…test. Oh...Uh…Good afternoon, everyone.
        I know that this is kind of an unusual cookie
        exchange this year. Due to someone's extremely
        selfish act, we have no Christmas cookies,
        anywhere in Frankincense. And that means we'll
        all have to find alternatives when it comes to
        Christmas treats this year.

Cut to a woman wiping away tears. Cut to another woman
blowing her nose.

                    MAYOR:
        Worse yet, I just received a call from Jimbo
        Louis, The CEO of CookieWorld Enterprises in
        Holly County and he had some worse news.

The crowd buzzes.
                    MAYOR:
        It seems… last night, someone burned the
        CookieWorld Factory to the ground.

The crowd gasps.

                    MAYOR:
        It was a five-alarm doozy. And, I'm sad to
        report, that all the cookies were, well,turned
        into lumps of coal, they were burnt so bad.

The crowd looks at each other and murmurs, a bit shocked.

                    MAYOR:
        Now, the Fire Inspector is saying that this was
        no accident. Somebody set that fire. And we have

reason to believe that those who did it may be
responsible for all the missing cookies too. I
invited Police Chief Williamson here to give us
some insight into what's going on. Chief?

William approaches the podium. He also tests the microphone
by tapping it with his hand.

                    WILLIAM:
Is this on? Is it? (FEEDBACK) Okay…Uh, hello,
everyone. Well, we have a pretty unusual
circumstance here. We have what we think could be
a sleeper cell of purps running an elite cookie
burglary ring that has affected just about every
household in Frankincense. Now, I don't know how
they're doing it but, believe you-me, we've got
everyone on the force investigating every single
instance of Cookie Crooking in town.

A villager in the audience speaks up as we see the crowd
that has gathered in front of the stage.

                 WOMAN IN CROWD 1:
Chief, could this be the work of one man?

                    WILLIAM:
Well, Betty, so far, we don't believe so. We
don't believe that anyone could visit so many
homes in one night without the help of…
(LAUGHING)Well…flying reindeer or something.

A murmur goes over the crowd. William gets a bit nervous.

                 REPORTER IN CROWD:
Chief, are you saying that this is the work of
Santa Claus?

                    WILLIAM:
What? No, no, no. We've completely ruled out
Santa. There is absolutely no evidence of any
reindeer or any illegal chimney activity
whatsoever.

A woman in the crowd speaks up.

                 WOMAN IN CROWD 2:
What are we going to do about the cookies?

> **ALL:**
> Yeah? What about the cookies? How are we gonna
> make it Christmas without the cookies? Etc.

> **WILLIAM:**
> Now folks, we know that this little setback
> changes a lot of your holiday plans but, as
> Frankincensians, adapting is what we do. It's
> what we're good at.

> **ALL:**
> I like egg nog. What happened to gingerbread? ETC

Cut back to Police Chief on stage. He's beginning to look a
little more nervous as sweat forms on his forehead and
upper lip. He tries to do some damage control.

> **WILLIAM:**
> Okay,. Calm down everyone. Look, we have a
> picture. This photo was taken through video
> surveillance. It's a little blurry, but we need
> to look at it closely. To see if it's somebody
> one of us could identify.

A giant photo of a shadowy figure in a blurry room goes on
the wall behind William. It's absolutely impossible to see
the person in the photo. The crowd murmurs again as they
try to make out what they're seeing—to no apparent avail.

> **WILLIAM:**
> Now, we've established a hefty reward for this
> criminal's whereabouts. And we're asking for
> volunteers to help bring these criminals to
> justice. See me if you'd like to help us out. In
> the meantime, have a great day. Mayor?

The mayor steps back to the podium.

> **MAYOR:**
> Thank you chief. And now…let's trade some
> biscuits, scones and danish, everyone!

The crowd is stunned silent momentarily.

                    MAYOR:
    Or other alternative baked goods?...Is that a
    bear claw? Ooh, is that a croissant?

Triumphant music plays. The Mayor taps the mic. The people
are suddenly a bit disparaged. They moan and slowly turn
and walk back to their display tables.

                                              -CUT

INT. SCHOOL COUNSELOR'S OFFICE—DAY (SNOWING OUTSIDE WINDOW)

Nat sits in a large chair across from an older gentleman
also in a large chair. The older man (JAHOSAPHAT IN
DISGUISE)slowly stirs hot cocoa in a mug overflowing with
marshmallows.

                    MR. GRISWOLD:
    So, Nathanial, tell me about this weird dream you
    had.

(Mr. Griswold is an elderly gentleman who is Nat's new
school psychologist. He is be speckled, bearded and bald
and bears a strange resemblance to Jahosaphat.

                    NAT:
    Well, I come downstairs and this bird man is
    stealing our Christmas cookies. And he seemed so
    familiar. Like I knew him. Then I wake up and all
    our cookies were gone. What is that? It's crazy,
    right?

                    MR. GRISWOLD:
    Well, Nat it's the nature of the holiday.
    Everyone looks at Christmas as this big, magical
    date on the calendar. But, for people like you
    and me, there's nothing magical about the 25th of
    December. I mean, I, myself, think Christmas is
    just a big waste of time. An empty promise from a
    father who was never there for me. Er…for you.

                    NAT:
    Mr. Griswold, I just wish I had my dad back.

                    MR. GRISWOLD:
Of course you do, Nat. You miss him and you want
Christmastime to pay for what they did to you.

                    NAT:
What? No. Christmas? This really doesn't have
anything to do with Christmas.

                    MR. GRISWOLD:
Doesn't it? You said yourself you wanted your dad
under the tree on Christmas morning.

                    NAT:
I…that's…no. I said I wanted him back.

                    MR. GRISWOLD:
So, in my opinion, your problem is Christmas.

                    NAT:
It is?

                    MR. GRISWOLD:
Of course it is.

                    NAT:
I don't like Christmas?

                    MR. GRISWOLD:
Don't like it? You despise it. You need to wipe
it from your life.

                    NAT:
I don't know if…

                    MR. GRISWOLD:
Nat, what if I told you that there was a way for
you to feel better about all this?

                    NAT:
Um.

                    MR. GRISWOLD:
Now,I work with a small group of people who have
been suffering from the same negative Christmas
issues you have.

Nat seems to be having an internal epiphany as he begins to get weirded out by Mr. Griswold. Mr. Griswold's mustache begins to look like it's falling off his face.

                    NAT:
You work with people who don't like Christmas?

                    MR. GRISWOLD:
Yes, we meet every so often to discuss this disgusting holiday. How much we…uh, *they* hate it. We talk about how worthless and how ridiculous it all is. And afterwards, we all feel much better.

                    NAT:
That seems a little weird.

                    MR. GRISWOLD:
Oh, it's not weird at all, son. And I think you would be a perfect fit for our group. Would you like to come to one of our meetings?

Mr. Griswold adjusts his mustache on his face, but it looks like it's losing its adhesiveness. Nat looks at it strangely and begins to suspect foul play at hand, but he's not quite sure if he's seeing things correctly.

                    NAT:
Um, with all due respect, Mr. Griswold, I appreciate your offer but I'm pretty busy that day.

                    MR. GRISWOLD:
I haven't mentioned a day yet, Nat.

                    NAT:
Er…right. What I mean is, I don't think that's something I can fit into the old schedule right now. I've got, uh…a lot going on, with homework and, uh…and soccer, and all…

                    MR. GRISWOLD:
Well, Nat, it's an open invitation. When you're ready, you know where I am.

Nat is beginning to really feel that Mr. Griswold has a darkness to him. He backs out of the room and into the hallway.

                    NAT:
Right. Because you'll be here. Okay. I gotta run.
I think I left something turned on at home. Like
the iron. Or, the oven. Or, the hair dryer. Or,
something. Thank you Mr. Griswold. For your time.
It was really helpful.

                 MR. GRISWOLD:
Okay, Nat. We've seemed to have really made
strides today. Perhaps we can schedule another
chat for next week?

Nat begins to hurry away.

                    NAT:
I um…I'll talk to the principal and get it in the
books. Okay. Right…Good talk!

Mr. Griswold watches Nat run down the hall. He talks to
himself as he adjusts his mustache.

                 Mr. Griswold:
That kid is hiding something. Hm. Weird.

                                              -CUT

INT. -JAHOSAPHAT'S MANSION--NIGHT

The Cookie Crook sits in his bird cage. He's sad. We can
tell that this has been how he's been treated for awhile.
Alone and forlorn, he reaches under the pillow on his cot
and removes the framed photo of Merry. He stares at the
photo then begins to sing.

                    TOM:
It's been too long since I saw you.
It's been too long since we danced
It's been too long since you said so long to me.
It's been too long since I kissed you
Underneath the mistletoe
But somehow you're a perfect memory
Be my Merry

Be my Merry

He quickly buries the photo back under his pillow as Ignacious appears, delivering a meal to him on a tray. Tom wipes away a tear. Ignacious pushes the tray under a gap in the bottom of the cage. Tom barely looks over at it. He holds his head low.

                    IGNACIOUS:
          Boss says you need to eat. Wants you to have
          enough energy to hit some of the houses on the
          outskirts of town tonight.

He points to the tray for the Cookie Crook.

                    IGNACIOUS:
          You know, between you and me, you working so
          hard's kinda making the rest of us look bad.
          Thinkin' you might want to pull it back a bit.

Tom looks up with one eye, but doesn't raise his head.

                    IGNACIOUS:
          I'm just sayin.' I mean, all those cookies you've
          managed to take and then the fire you set?
          Genius. But it kind of casts a negative light on
          the rest of us. Like we're not doing enough to
          ruin the holidays and…

Tom finally looks up. He stares at Ignacious.

                    TOM:
          Wait…Wait a minute…Back up…Did you say, "Fire?"

                    IGNACIOUS:
          Yeah. At the CookieWorld Factory. All the
          chocolate chips melted. All the sugar turned to
          syrup. All the sprinkles turned into a hot mess.
          A colorful mess, but a hot mess. You've
          eliminated the possibility of any Christmas
          cookies being produced for like, years.

                    TOM:
          Whoa, whoa, whoa. I didn't start any fire.

                    IGNACIOUS:
Uh. Sure you didn't. Look, Jahosaphat's gonna
systematically wipe out Christmas with us or
without us. So, what difference does it make?

                    TOM:
It makes a big difference. I don't want to be
blamed for something I didn't do. Stealing
cookies is one thing, but setting fire to a
factory? I think that kind of crosses the line!

                    IGNACIOUS:
Well, yeah. It's pretty over-the-top. But at
least nobody was hurt.

                    TOM:
Good. But, the idea of it. Horrible.

                    IGNACIOUS:
Right?

                    TOM:
Yes! You know, it's interesting…you've got a
pretty good sense of right or wrong, Iggy. What's
your story?

                    IGNACIOUS:
My story? Well, uh. I used to be a reindeer but
the other reindeer used to laugh and call me
names. But I did have a nose that glowed…

                    TOM:
Uh. That sounds kinda familiar. Are you sure
about that?

                    IGNACIOUS:
No. I'm not. Ya know, I think I was a snowman
built by children who placed a magic hat upon my…

                    TOM:
Mmm. I feel like I've heard that one before too.

                    IGNACIOUS:
I was a furry green outcast?

                    TOM:
That actually might be a trademark infringement.

                    IGNACIOUS:
You know, come to think of it, I don't know my
story. I don't remember it.

                    TOM:
Now, how can you randomly recall all those other
stories, but you don't know your own?

                    IGNACIOUS:
(Matter-of-Factly) Oh. My mind is scrambled mush.
Jahosaphat says it's because of the anti-
Christmas serum. It makes you forget everything.
It's effects wear off every couple of months.
That's why the boss keeps upping our doses.

                    TOM:
Wait…What?

                    IGNACIOUS:
Oh yeah. It's in the food he serves us. Mixed in
about once a month. We don't even know we're
getting' it. But, it works like a charm. Right? I
mean, when's the last time you remembered
anything?

                    TOM:
I really don't remember—now that I think about
it.

Tom counts on his fingers. Stops after two, frustrated.

                    IGNACIOUS:
See? Like a charm.

                    TOM:
But, wait. He's giving us this serum without us
knowing about it?

                    IGNACIOUS:
Of course. He can do whatever he wants. He's the
boss. Duh.
                    TOM:
I know, but I don't think this is very fair.
You know what? I'm not eating it.

Tom slides the tray back under the cage bars to Ignacious. Ignacious looks baffled.

                    IGNACIOUS:
          Hey, c'mon! You gotta eat it, cookie dude.

He slides the tray back to Tom, who slides it back again.

                    TOM:
          Nope.

                    IGNACIOUS:
          C'mon, man. I think I'll get in trouble if you
          don't eat it.

                    TOM:
          I'm sorry about that, but Iggy, I'm not going to
          eat that and be under the influence of this Anti-
          Christmas Serum, or whatever.

Ignacious slides it back.

                    IGNACIOUS:
          You have to!

                    TOM:
          Don't you get it, Ignacious. If we don't eat,
          maybe we won't get our dose. Then, maybe all our
          memories will come back.

Tom picks up the tray, then dumps it in the trash can in his cage.

                    IGNACIOUS:
          You don't know that for sure. It's different for
          all of us.

                    TOM:
          What are you saying?

                    IGNACIOUS:
          Okay…this serum…Everybody reacts differently to
          their doses. I require a bit more because I'm a
          bigger guy. It could take me years to get it all
          out of my system and get my memories back, once I
          go cold turkey—eh, pardon the pun.

Ignacious looks at Tom's turkey wings. Tom looks down at them.

>   TOM:
>   I get it. But, doesn't that bother you? don't you
>   miss the memories? Don't you wonder who you were
>   before? What you did before? What life was like
>   before?

>   IGNACIOUS:
>   I really haven't thought about it at all. Er,
>   maybe I have. I don't remember.

>   TOM:
>   Are you kidding me? A guy like you could've been
>   something in your previous life. Something
>   amazing. A captain of industry. A cruise ship
>   entertainer. A coffee barista.

>   IGNACIOUS:
>   Oh, come on. That's a little far fetched. What
>   would make anyone think I could've been any of
>   those things?

>   TOM:
>   Well, look at you. You look uh…prosperous.

Tom acknowledges the servant's belly. He suddenly notices something written on his hand. We push it in to see the numbers, 12-25-20.

>   TOM:
>   Uh…yeah…and you've got that something-something
>   that says, "success." You know what it is?

>   IGNACIOUS:
>   What?

>   TOM:
>   It's your…uh. I don't know… your character.
>   You've got character!

>   IGNACIOUS:
>   Aw…you don't know what you're talking about.

>   TOM:
>   (SINGING)

Character.
You've got character.
You've got charm, you're debonair, you've got
pizzazz.
Character. Like a real good narrator.
You're strong, authoritative, with a touch of
razzmatazz
And when you speak the whole wide world will
listen in.
'Cause you don't just shine, you glitter, and
you're glistenin'.
Yes, you've got Character. Too much to bear-actor
You've got that thing, that ring-a-ding, that
I'll address.
Character…Sweet like pear nectar.

                    IGNACIOUS:
(TALKING) Whoa, that's a stretch.

                    TOM:
If you were a CEO, my gosh, you'd be a fat
success—no offense.

                    IGNACIOUS:
(TALKING) None taken.

                    TOM:
And when you lead, the oth-er workers will unite.
They'll 'preciate your thinking
And your trademark overbite.

Ignacious looks beyond Tom and catches a glimpse of the
photo of Merry on the table next to his cot. He's staring
at it. Tom reaches out and turns the combination lock to
12. Then stands in front of the photo, to get Ignacious'
attention back on him.

                    TOM:
Yes, you've got character
C'mon, don't stare at her.

Tom picks up the photo and puts it in his vest. He has
turned his back on Ignacious. He looks over his shoulder to
turn the lock to 25. He hands Ignacious a wood recorder
with the other hand.

                    TOM:
          There's something special 'bout the way you go
          through life.
          Character. Like a pretty fair actor.
          You play the part like a world class flautist
          plays the fife.

Ignacious plays the recorder like an old pro—as a solo
within the song. While Ignacious is lost in the music, Tom
has opened the combination lock. He has also moved out of
the cage and has moved Ignacious inside of it—while the
servant continues his solo on the recorder.
                    TOM:
          And when you're on your game
          It's like you're on a stage
          You're so naïve you'll end up
          Locked inside my cage.
          You and your character.
          My cell inheritor..
          You might believe you're special,
          Just like 'ol Santa Claus.
          But your char-act-er
          Could also be just one…
          Of your character's flaws!

Ignacious doesn't realize that he's been duped by Tom. He
puts his hands on the bars of the cage.

                    IGNACIOUS:
          Well, that's a nice complement. I appreciate the
          sentiment. And I thank you.

                    TOM:
          Don't mention it.

Tom walks off. Ignacious finally comes to understand what
just happens. He sits down on the cot, defeated, and begins
to eat the meal he brought to Tom.

                    IGNACIOUS:
          Hey…wait a minute!

He dips a spoon into a bowl of pudding. And begins to eat.

                    IGNACIOUS:
          Darn it! How can I be so stupid? Wait…Mmm.
          Tapioca.

-CUT

EXT. FRANKINSENCE POLICE HEADQUARTERS—MORNING

William is addressing a large group of angry villagers
outside the police station. He stands in front of a white
board that maps out various locations in town where the
Cookie Crook has been seen. The locations are connected by
red yarn. There's yarn all over the map. The crowd is
dressed for a hunt.

                    CHIEF WILLIAM:
          Ladies and gentlemen, I want to thank you for
          joining me in this man hunt. These cookies are
          important to us and so is the idea of bringing
          this criminal—or criminals—to justice.

Cut to some of the people in the crowd looking at each
other.

                    CHIEF WILLIAM:
          Remember: we work with the buddy system. Stay
          with your buddy at all times. Now, we're
          scheduled to go until 5. So, synchronize your
          watches and let's meet right back here If you
          discover anything, use your walkie-talkie to
          contact me or one of the three deputies. Don't
          try to be a hero. We're a search and rescue
          party. None of you are qualified to take any
          police action. Leave that to the professionals.

A villager raises his hand. He's standing next to two
large, bearded buddies who look like they all just stepped
out of *Duck Dynasty*.

                    CHIEF WILLIAM:
          Chaz…a question?

                    CHAZ:
          Yessir. Let's say me 'an the boys here find the
          source of this cookie crookin'. And let's say
          we're able to lead you to the suspects, and you
          recover the stolen merchandise. Is there any kind

of reward we should be aware of hitherto and henceforth?

Chaz (50-ish), is a local yokel. A bearded, camouflage-wearing hunter type with a heart of gold but a bit naïve. He's ready to do anything for his town.

                    CHIEF WILLIAM:
          That's a good point, Chaz. Truth be told, his
          honor, the Mayor, has offered a nice reward for
          information leading to the recovery of the
          cookies and an even bigger one for bringing these
          creeps to justice.

The crowd gets excited.

                    MAN IN CROWD:
          We need those cookies found now!

                    ALL:
          Incredible! Count us in! Etc.

Suddenly, through the hullabaloo, we hear a howling sound. The townsfolk look annoyed, put their fingers in their ears. We cut to see that the sound is an old, craggy man (actually Jehoshaphat in disguise). The old man has transformed himself with a little makeup and prosthetics to resemble a dog.

                    JAHOSAPHAT:
          Hoowwwl!

The crowd stops buzzing as all their attention shifts to Jahosaphat, in the back of the crowd, sitting in a folding chair and whittling.

                    JAHOSAPHAT:
          Yep…they call me "Billy The Bloodhound." Spent my
          whole life solving mysteries because I could find
          things nobody else could. Like a Bloodhound.
          Hoowwl! (Cough-cough) Anyway, I've been a private
          eye for years. Made a career out of sniffing out
          crime, and fetching stuff. And I can find just
          about anything. I've found things that have been
          lost and things that have been stolen. And some
          things that weren't lost and weren't stolen. I've
          found coins in couch cushions, dollars in my

jeans and I've even found trouble—on more than
one occasion—point is, I'm a finder. I'm a
rescuer. I'm like a rescue dog.

                    CHAZ:
Uh, I thought you said you were like a
bloodhound?

                    JAHOSAPHAT:
I *am* like a bloodhound!

                    CHAZ:
But, Bloodhounds ain't rescue dogs.

                    JAHOSAPHAT:
Sure they are.

                    CHAZ:
Well, no. Actually, a St. Bernard is more like a
rescue dog.

                    JAHOSAPHAT:
What's the difference?

                    CHAZ:
I'd say about 70 lbs. St. Bernard's can get
pretty big. And they have more fur because…

                    JAHOSAPHAT:
(FRUSTRATED) …Aw, I find stuff and I rescue
stuff! And if you want to find these cookies? You
hire me. But, it's not gonna be easy. There's
lots of 'em missin'. But, I'll find every one of
these delicious Christmas treats. Take you right
to 'em and the bandits who took 'em. And you'll,
in turn, pay me the reward yer offerin' plus <u>this</u>
for my services.

He hands a slip of paper to the Police Chief who opens it.

                    JAHOSAPHAT:
That's how you get your cookies back.

The Chief opens the paper. He's surprised and finds it a
bit ridiculous. Actually laughs a bit.

CHIEF WILLIAM:
Ho. Whoa! With all due respect, we can't pay
anyone this much to find Christmas cookies. Not
even a bird dog like yourself.

JAHOSAPHAT:
Bloodhound!

CHIEF WILLIAM:
Whatever.

JAHOSAPHAT:
That's fine, Chief. But I don't know if the good
people of Frankincense would want another part of
Christmas to disappear. Like egg nog…or candy
canes did on *your watch*. That's won't sit well
with anyone come election time.

CARL (VILLAGER):
The old dog makes a good point, Chief. Frankly,
you don't want Frankincensians to be incensed
again. Hey, a play on words! High five!

Carl lifts his hand for a high five from a guy next to him.
The guy obliges him. Carl grins.

CHIEF WILLIAM:
C'mon, Carl, this guy's holding us hostage.

JAHOSAPHAT:
Call it what you will, Chief. But, your community
needs you now. And I'm like your border collie
who can wrangle those cookies right back into the
hands of their rightful owners.

CHAZ:
Ugh! I'm confused again, I thought you were a
bloodhound.

JAHOSAPHAT:
Semantics!

CHIEF WILLIAM:
Well…considering the circumstances…I guess I'll
put it up to vote. Who thinks this man should be
hired to find our Christmas cookies?

People in the crowd look at each other. Slowly but surely,
lots of hands go up in the air.

                    CHIEF WILLIAM:
Well…okay…Find our cookies and help bring the
criminals to justice. I'll talk to the mayor and
we'll pay you what you require.

                    JAHOSAPHAT:
You won't regret this, good people of
Frankincense! I'll track these thieves down like
a bull dog.

                    CROWD:
A bloodhound!

                    JAHOSAPHAT:
Yes! Bloodhound!

                                        -CUT

INT. -MERRY'S HOUSE—NEXT MORNING

Nat is scurrying about his room, getting his winter clothes
on. Maddy looks worried about him as he scrounges about.
Their grandma is in the living room watching a show on tv.

                    MADDY:
How are you going to find them?

                    NAT:
I'll find them. Don't worry about it.

                    MADDY:
Well, you can't just go by yourself.

                    NAT:
I can so.

                    MADDY:
Well, I'm telling mom, when she gets home from
Christmas shopping.

                    NAT:
You can't tell mom. I'm grounded still. She won't
let me leave the house! And if you do, I'll have
to tell her about your report card.

                    MADDY:
What report card?

                    NAT:
The one under you're hiding under your mattress
that came in the mail yesterday. Because of a
certain grade in something that rhymes with bath.

                    MADDY:
(GASPS) How did you know..?

                    NAT:
I know about everything…I'm loco.

He uses his finger to draw a circle in the air around the
side of his head.

                    MADDY:
Ugh! Nat!

                    NAT:
Look. I'm being careful. I'm taking a backpack
full of supplies, just in case I run into
trouble.

He opens up a backpack and starts to dig through it,
showing Maddy what he's got as he names the items.

                    NAT:
I've got a flashlight, a canister of bear
repellent, my Swiss Army knife, water, a bunch of
energy bars, The Cookie Crook Hunter's Survival
Guide, my phone and a rechargeable
battery…everything I need to do this.

He momentarily takes a teddy bear out of his pack and then
puts the bear back in the back pack when Maddy sees it.

                    MADDY:
Was that your Teddy Bear?

NAT:
What? Uh…no. Er, it must've fallen in when I
packed the trail mix.

Nat takes the teddy bear out for a moment, then puts it
right back in the backpack.

NAT:
I can bring this guy to justice, Maddy. And I can
get the cookies back!

MADDY:
Maybe. But, I don't want anything to happen to
you!

NAT:
I'm gonna be fine.

Maddy grabs a coat and begins to put it on.

MADDY:
I know you will be. Know why?

NAT:
Why?

MADDY:
Because I'm going with you.

NAT:
Oh-no you're not.

MADDY:
Then I am telling Mom. And I don't care if you
tell her about my report card! And I mean that!

NAT:
Eh!.. You'd better get some gloves.

MADDY:
Whoo-hoo! Whoever crooked these cookies is about
to face the music, thanks to the Buckleberry
Twins! Fist bump, bro-hammer!

Maddy sticks her fist out to bump her brother's. Nat leaves
her hanging. She pulls her fist back and "blows it up."

                              NAT:
          We're leaving in five minutes. Tell grandma we're
          going outside and I'll write a note for mom.

Maddy races out of the room to get ready.

                                                      -CUT

EXT. —ON THE SIDE OF A SNOWY MOUNTAIN—AFTERNOON

The Old Man is using his nose to lead a group of Villagers
up the mountain.

                         JAHOSAPHAT:
          Almost there! I'm getting a good reading. Nose,
          don't fail me now! Right?

                         POLICE CHIEF:
          You'd better be right about this.

The Villagers look exhausted.

                              CHAZ:
          Yeah. I'm tired of all these false alarms!

                         JAHOSAPHAT:
          Patience. (SNIFF!) There! Over there. At the
          opening on the side of the mountain.

                         POLICE CHIEF:
          You mean that cave?

                         JAHOSAPHAT:
          Don't question a shepherd like me! To the cave,
          friends!

The police chief rolls his eyes and looks at a deputy
nearby.

                         POLICE CHIEF:
          I hope we're not being dogged by this guy.

The group trudges on through the snow, toward the cave.

                                                      -CUT

INT. -JAHOSAPHAT'S MANSION—EVENING

Tom is hiding in a hallway as the other servants are
walking about. He tiptoes across the floor and hides behind
various plants, pillars and curtains as he tries to get to
the front door. Once again, the paintings seem to follow
him with their eyes.

                                                    -CUT

INT. -JAHOSAPHAT'S MANSION CAGE ROOM—EVENING

Ignacious is in the Cookie Crook's cage as The Humbug
Brothers (Harry and Herb), walk into the room. They see
Ignacious, casually enjoying a bowl of pudding.

                    HARRY:
          What the heck? Iggy?

                    HERB:
          Where's the turkey dude?

                    IGNACIOUS:
          He tricked me! He told me I was charming, and he
          tricked me!

                    HARRY:
          Are you eating his figgy pudding?

                    IGNACIOUS:
          It's tapioca. Let me outta here, fellas, I gotta
          find him before the boss gets back or I'm doomed!

Ignacious has a pudding mustache. He's a messy eater.

                    HERB:
          Are you kidding? If the Old Man gets back and the
          Cookie Crook is gone, we're all doomed.

                        IGNACIOUS:
                  Oh! It's all my fault!

The Humbug Brothers jimmy the lock on the cage to let their
cohort out. While Herb works the lock, Harry speaks into a
small speaker on his shoulder to call in the crime.

                          HARRY:
            Azar! We've got a code red. I repeat, a code red!

                                                    -CUT

INT. A CONTROL ROOM SOMEWHERE IN THE BOWELS OF JAHOSAPHAT'S
MANSION—SAME EVENING

Azar is in front of a wall of video screens, all showing
various parts of the mansion. Melky is at the control
board. Both are wearing headsets to communicate. Melky is
reading a manual then, turns on a siren. We cut to various
shots of sirens lighting up all around the mansion. We see
cameras in the eyes of people in the paintings go on and
start panning back and forth. Azar shouts out orders to the
others in the control room.

                          AZAR:
            Code Red! Code Red! What's a code red? Oh..an
            escape! Ah…Give me camera 13!

The main video screen shows the view from camera 13. We see
nothing, just an empty hallway.

                          AZAR:
            Nothing…Give me 14!

The main video switches to another view.

                          AZAR:
            Nothing…Now 15…Where are you, you turkey-winged
            cookie-crooking freak?

As the alarms continue to sound, we cut back to the Cookie
Crook under a stairway. Some guards run by him but he stays
hidden.

                                                          -CUT

EXT. -ON A COLORFUL PATH MADE OF COOKIES RUNNING THROUGH
THE VILLAGE OF FRANKINCENSE.

We see Nat and Maddy following the path through backyards,
over fences. Then, the path takes them outside city limits.
We see them pass a scarecrow by a subtle yellow brick road,
nearly covered in snow. They trudge into the woods,
following a path of colorful cookies that winds its way
through the woods.

                         MADDY:
              This is too weird.

                          NAT:
              It's pretty amazing.

                         MADDY:
              I have to admit, I'm pretty scared, Nat.

                          NAT:
              Well, sure you are. You're a girl.

                         MADDY:
              What's that supposed to mean?

                          NAT:
              Well, it's a proven fact that girls scare easier
              than boys.

                         MADDY:
              Oh, really?

                          NAT:
              Oh yeah. It's in your genes. It's proven
              scientifically. Look…
              (SINGING)Boys were made for being brave,
              On that you can rely on.

> Girls are like the little lamb,
> And boys are like a li-on.
> Someday I'll grow a handsome mane.

                    MADDY:
Ohmigosh, that'd be so lame.

                    NAT:
Boys don't scare so easily.

                    MADDY:
So, prove your stupid case to me…

                    NAT:
(TALKING) I will…
(SINGING) 65 percent of ghost hunters are boys.

Nat turns his back for a second and walks toward a tree.
When he gets near it, Maddy jumps out from behind the tree
and scares him.
                    MADDY:

(TALKING) Boo!

                    NAT:
(SINGING) Ah! 73 percent of storm chasers are
boys.

Nat reaches into his backpack and pulls out an umbrella. He
puts it up. Just then, Maddy throws a snowball at a tree
branch, the snow rains down on the umbrella.

                    MADDY:
(TALKING) You're a big bag of wind.

                    NAT:
What do croc hunters have in common, other than
what they most enjoy?

Nat puts the umbrella down and uses it to poke a shrub
nearby that looks like an alligator. The shrub snaps at him
and he jumps back. Maddy giggles.

                    MADDY:
(TALKING) What?

                    NAT:
        They're boys. Yessir, they're boys.

Maddy crosses her arms and looks unconvinced.

                    MADDY:
        (TALKING) I'm gonna need more data.

Nat pulls out his phone and Googles something.

                    NAT:
        I'm pretty sure most of your best surgeons are
        boys.

                    MADDY:
        (TALKING) That can't be fact checked.

Nat jumps on a log that looks like a horse. He takes off
his hat and waves it like a cowboy on a bronco.

                    NAT:
        All of the world's cowboys are boys. (Yee-haw!)

                    MADDY:
        (TALKING) I'm gonna give you that one.

Nat walks to a stump that's sticking out of the ground that
looks like a podium. He stands behind it as if giving his
inauguration speech.

                    NAT:
        And what were all the presidents when they were
        young and played with toys?
        They were boys. Yessir, they're boys…

                    MADDY:
        We're working on that.

Nat sits down on another stump and begins to write a
scientific equation in the snow with a stick.

                    NAT:
        Most of your best scientists are boys.

Maddy looks down at the equation Nat has written and shakes her head, "no." She takes her own stick and crosses out the equation.

                    MADDY:
          E equals MC wrong.

                     NAT:
          Most of your best archeologists are boys.

Nat sees something in the snow that Maddy crossed her stick through. He pulls a spade out of his backpack and begins to dig, quickly. He picks up an item, revealling that it's a dinosaur skull made out of snow. Maddy, just as quickly, smashes the snow skull as Nat holds it in his hand.

                    MADDY:
          I'm not digging these lies.

                     NAT:
          Who's louder and more prouder when it comes to
          making noise?

                    MADDY:
          I'll agree on that one.

                     NAT:
          The boys. Yessir, the boys.

Now looks directly at Nat.

                    MADDY:
          Okay, I think I see where you're going with this…
          (SINGING) 100% of those who leave the seat up are
          boys.

We cut to Nat who peeks out from behind a tree. It looks as if he's been pee-ing.

                     NAT:
          Not this time.

                    MADDY:
          Gross! (SINGING)100% of those who tell if
          something's clean by smell are boys.

Nat smells his armpits/shirt.

NAT:
(SNIFF) It's clean!

As they continue to walk, Nat reaches up to grab a low-hanging tree branch. He pulls it then lets it go, showering Maddy with snow.

MADDY:
And who will just do anything, as long as it annoys? You boys…Yessir, you boys.

She brushes the snow off of herself.

NAT:
You're going to go there?

Nat laughs. Then, he picks his nose. Maddy catches him picking.

MADDY:
99.9% of nose pickers are boys.
(TALKING) Wave when you get to the bridge.

Nat looks over at his sister and doesn't get the joke.

NAT:
Huh?

MADDY:
99% of bathtub rings come from boys.

NAT:
You debate dirty!

MADDY:
98% of Joes and Franks and Hanks and Roys…are boys. Yessir, they're boys.

NAT:
You have your thoughts, that's obvious, but mine's the real McCoy.

The two kids keep jumping in front of each other—like a big finish—exclaiming their lines each time.

MADDY:
Boys. Typical.

                    NAT:
          Boys. Honorable.

                    MADDY:
          Boys. Comical.

                    NAT:
          Boys. Unequivocal.

                    MADDY:
          Boys. Pathological.

                    NAT:
          Boys. Astronomical.

                    MADDY:
          Boys. Egotistical.

                    NAT:
          Boys. Undeniable.

                    BOTH:
          Boys. Yessir, they're boys!

The song finishes and the kids carry on.

                    MADDY:
          C'mon, Nat. Admit that you're a little freaked
          out right now.

                    NAT:
          Are you serious?   This is a piece of cake.

                    MADDY:
          Well, this piece of cake sure would be a lot
          better with some cookies on it. See what I did
          there?

                    NAT:
          Very fun…

The kids' conversation is interrupted by a strange sound.

                    NAT:
          Wait…Uh…do you hear something?

                    NAT:
          It's coming from that tree!

The colorful cookie path seems to end around the tree. The
siren noise gets a bit louder as they approach it. They put
their ears to the tree and the sound gets even louder. They
begin to feel the tree.

                    MADDY:
          It's inside the tree! The sound is on the inside!

                    NAT:
          So weird. It's like, echo-y.

Nat walks around the tree to see a stick sticking out of
the ground. He pushes the stick down toward the ground and
a door slides open near Maddy on the other side of the
tree. She turns her head toward the opening in the tree and
sees a red light going on and off and a stairway leading
downward.

                    MADDY:
          Nat! You gotta see this!

Nat comes hurriedly around the tree and gasps.

                    NAT:
          It's a stairway. This is it, Maddy!

Nat begins to walk through the door. Maddy grabs his arm
and pulls him back.

                    MADDY:
          Whoa, whoa, whoa…you're not thinking about going
          down there, are you?

                    NAT:
          No. I'm *not* thinking about *me* going down there.
          I'm thinking about *us* going down there.

                    MADDY:
          I'm going with you…down a strange, secret
          stairway? In a spooky tree? With weird sounds?

                    NAT:
          Or, you're staying up here in this dark, scary
          woods all by yourself.

                    MADDY:
          Okay! Let's do this thing!

The kids begin to walk down the steps of the tree.

                                        -CUT

INT. THE BUCKLEBERRY HOUSE - LATE AFTERNOON

Merry walks in the kitchen door with Christmas presents and
puts them down on the counter. Her mother is making dinner
while she watches a soap opera on the tv.

                    MERRY:
          Mom? How'd it go? Where are the kids?

                    MARGARET:
          Oh, those little angels went out to make a
          snowman.

                    MERRY:
          Out back?

                    MARGARET:
          Yes.

Merry looks out the back patio double door and we see two
snow men, wearing kid clothing.

                    MERRY:
          Mom, they're not out there.

                    MARGARET:
          Oh, of course they are, Merry.

                    MERRY:
          They're not in the backyard, Mom!

                    MARGARET:
          Oh, the little stinkers are right there.

Margaret points to the two snow men in the backyard.

                    MERRY:
    Mom, those are snow men. What's this?

Merry sees a note on the countertop. She reads it.

                    MERRY:
    "Dear Mom. We've gone to get the cookies back.
    We'll be home before supper. Maddy is going with
    me. I know nothing about her report card. Love,
    Nat…" Oh, no!
Margaret takes her phone out and begins to dial.

                    MERRY:
    Mom!?

                    MARGARET:
    Let's not panic, Merry. I'm calling your father.

                    MERRY:
    Oh, no…
                                              -CUT

EXT. -EARLY EVENING OUTSIDE THE FRONT OF WHAT LOOKS LIKE A
CAVE.

Jahosaphat (The Bloodhound) has now led the cookie recovery
team to the front of the cave. The Chief looks down at his
phone.

                    POLICE CHIEF:
    Darn it!

                    JAHOSAPHAT:
    What's the matter, Chief?

                    POLICE CHIEF:
    Ugh! No bars. Cell phone's worthless up here.

                    JAHOSAPHAT:
    Well, let's get in the cave. At lease it will
    protect us from the wind and the cold.

The rescue team walks into the cave. Jahosaphat allows the others to enter before him.

> JAHOSAPHAT:
> Now, be careful. Watch your step. A little further…

Jahosaphat reaches up to the side of a big rock. He pulls a lever and a large gate closes at the opening of the cave. He's still on the outside, the others are locked inside.

> POLICE CHIEF:
> Wait…What is this?

> JAHOSAPHAT:
> This is called the old switcheroo, Chief. And you all fell for it, hook, line and sinker! Ha!

Jahosaphat takes off his fake nose and hair, revealing himself.

> POLICE CHIEF:
> Jahosaphat B. Higgins the 3rd?!

> JAHOSAPHAT:
> In the flesh.

> COLBY:
> Wait... *the* Jahosaphat Higgins who disappeared what, twenty years ago? I wondered what happened to him!

> POLICE CHIEF:
> Well, obviously, he became a fool. Thinking he could trick the Police Chief of Frankincense. Not exactly one of the wise men.

> JAHOSAPHAT:
> Oh yeah? Who's gonna be the wiser when you're a Cop-sicle…Ha! Get it? A Cop-sicle? Because you're a policeman and it's cold outside?

The Police Chief and the others look at each other.

> POLICE CHIEF:
> Yeah. I get it. Hilarious. Now, I'd suggest you let us out of here.

JAHOSAPHAT:
Oh, no. You're not getting out! Tomorrow's
Christmas Eve and all of you will be spending the
holiday together. Caveman style! And, with you
out of the way, my master plan to ruin Christmas
in Frankincense will be hatched. Now…I hate to
run, but there's only one more stealing day! And
I've got so much fun to take away!

POLICE CHIEF:
Stealing day? Wait a minute, are you the one
behind the stealing of the cookies?

JAHOSAPHAT:
I can't say I am and I can't say I am not. But
you know what I can say?

CHAZ:
What?

JAHOSAPHAT:
Merry Nothing! Because that's what Christmas is
gonna be when me and my army are done with it!

COLBY:
Did he just say, "Merry Nothing," Chief? What
does that mean by that?

POLICE CHIEF:
I think it means, we might be in trouble.

JAHOSAPHAT:
Bad guy…out!

COLBY:
Did he just say, "Bad guy…out?"

POLICE CHIEF:
Yep. Did that too.

Jahosaphat slams his foot on the ground and a circular,
silver saucer sled flies up in the air. Jahosaphat catches
it, jumps on it and begins to surf/sled down the side of
the mountain. Chaz is up against the bars of the jail/cave.

                    CHAZ:
     Well, he does seem like one bad guy. (AWESTRUCK)
     But, he's a fantastic sledder.

We see Jahosaphat hit a bump on the snowy mountain and, X-
Games-style, land a perfect gainer, continuing down the
mountain.

                                              -CUT

INT. INSIDE THE STAIRCASE WITHIN THE TREE NAT AND MADDY
DISCOVERED - SAME AFTERNOON

Nat and Maddy are making their way down a stairway in the
tree. They open a door at the end of the stairs and walk
into a huge storage facility. Lining the walls are candy
canes, barrels marked, "Egg Nog," bins full of single
Christmas light bulbs, gingerbread houses, piles of
cookies, plus, shelves of Christmas albums, nativity
scenes, blo-mold character lights, etc. It's full of all
the Christmas things that Jahosaphat's gang have stolen.

                    MADDY:
     What is this place?

                    NAT:
     It's some kind of storage area.

We see around the entire space from the POV of Nat and
Maddy.

                    MADDY:
     For Santa Claus? Nat, are we at the North Pole?

                    NAT:
     I don't think so. Whoever owns this place isn't
     making stuff. They're taking stuff.

                    MADDY:
     Why would someone steal all this Christmas stuff?

                    NAT:
     I have no idea. But, I haven't seen things like
     this since we were little.

                    MADDY:
     Ooh, you're right. We haven't had egg nog, candy
     canes or gingerbread since we were little. I
     didn't think they made them anymore. Look at
     that!

Maddy directs Nat's attention over to a robotic machine
pounding out fruit cakes one at a time. Then to a pile of
cookies.

                     NAT:
     Ugh. Gross. Anyway, I bet whoever took all this
     stuff is probably the same people who stole all
     of the… The Christmas cookies!

Nat points to the pile of cookies and the weighing machine
nearby.
                                                    -CUT

INT. THE CONTROL ROOM -MOMENTS LATER

Azar is panicking, sitting in a control room rotating
chair. One particular screen in the bottom of the video
screen wall catches his eye. Melky and Gaspar are in the
room, along with a young operative working the board.

                    AZAR:
     Wait a minute…pull up camera 36…

A worker presses a button on a control board and camera
36's view comes on the big screen. We clearly see Nat and
Maddy walking through the storage facility.

                    AZAR:
     What do we have here? Intruders in the storage
     area?

George looks up at Azar.

                    GEORGE:
     Ooh. I think that's a code green, sir.

(George is a brainy kid who works as a controller in Azar's
control room)

                    AZAR:
          I know what it is, ya darn Millennial!

He speaks into his receiver on his shoulder.

                    AZAR:
          Attention. We now have a code green in the
          storage area. Repeat, a code green in the storage
          area. Code Red in the main wing, code green in
          the storage area!

He looks over at the worker who is a bit green himself.

                    AZAR:
          What's the matter, son?

                    GEORGE:
          I'm nervous, sir? We've never had a code red, or
          a code green.

                    AZAR:
          So.

                    GEORGE:
          Those two together could lead to a code brown.

                    AZAR:
          Well, there are extra uniform pants in the
          drawer, if you need 'em. Let's get back to
          searching for the Cookie Crook. Melky…Gaspar…come
          with me!

The three walk out the door. We see cuts to various alarms
going off and siren lights now flashing red and green.

                                                  -CUT

INT. UNDER A STAIRWAY SOMEWHERE IN THE MANSION -AT THE SAME
TIME

Tom watches Edison walk by the stairwell. As she goes, she reaches up to twist the light bulbs high up in the ceiling, turning them on. Unaware that Tom is nearby, she turns a corner. Tom slowly slinks out from under the stairs and quickly moves down the hall in the opposite direction, looking over his shoulder the entire way.

                                                        -CUT

INT. MERRY'S HOUSE —NIGHTTIME

Merry is a bit distraught. Her phone rings and she answers it.

                    MERRY:
          Hello, Kathryn. Hello?

                    KATHRYN:
          (Through phone) Merry? Ohmigosh, Merry, I heard
          about Nat and Maddy. What can I do to help?

                    MERRY:
          I don't know. My dad has disappeared too. I don't
          know what's going on.

                    KATHRYN:
          Well, the girls and I are coming over. Don't
          worry. They're probably fine. All of them. Stay
          put, we'll be right over!

                    SFX:
          CLICK OF PHONE HANGING UP.

Merry looks over at a photo of her husband and children when they were all younger. She holds the picture close to her heart.

                                                        -CUT

INT. THE HILL SIDE OF A SNOWY HILL —SAME EVENING

Jahosaphat speed sleds down the hill. He puts an earphone in his ear (it's attached to his phone). He can now hear the team back at the mansion. We split the screen to show Azar as Jahosaphat overhears his conversation.

                    AZAR (VO):
          I don't care what it takes! We've got a missing
          bird, an empty cage and intruders in the stock
          room. We've got to get this place back to normal
          before the boss comes back!

                    JAHOSAPHAT:
          Azar? Is that you? What did you just say?

                    AZAR:
          Oh, hey, boss? That you boss? You-ah…you get rid
          of the sheriff and the search party?

                    JAHOSAPHAT:
          Yes, Azar. It's handled. But the more important
          question is, "What's going on there?!"

                    AZAR:
          Here? Uh…not much.(ASIDE: Code Black! Code
          Black!)

Azar puts a hand over the walkie-talkie and whisper-yells to the workers with him.

                    JAHOSAPHAT:
          I'm gone for just a couple hours and you're in
          peril?

                    AZAR:
          Well, sir, the Cookie Crook got out of his
          cage…and…

                    JAHOSAPHAT:
          What? How?

                    AZAR:
          He tricked us, sir. But, he's still in the
          building. Edison is looking for him now. If
          anyone can find him, it's her.

                    JAHOSAPHAT:
          Well, so, we're in a code red?

> AZAR:
> That's true, sir. And we've got intruders. A
> couple of kids who've snuck into the storage
> facility.

> JAHOSAPHAT:
> Wait…what?

> AZAR:
> Two kids got into the storage area…

> JAHOSAPHAT:
> That's a code green, General Azar. And I'm not
> very happy about it.

> AZAR:
> I understand, sir. And I assure you we're taking
> care of that too.

> JAHOSAPHAT:
> And I assure _you_ that someone will be held
> accountable for this!

> AZAR:
> Yessir.

> JAHOSAPHAT:
> Find that Cookie Crook! Capture those kids!

> AZAR:
> Yessir! Right away, sir!

Jahosaphat hangs up on the call as Azar is pushed out of
the frame.

> JAHOSAPHAT:
> Idiots!

-CUT

INT. STORAGE ROOM OF JAHOSAPHAT'S MANSION—MOMENTS LATER

> NAT:
> Look at all these Christmas cookies!

Nat looks over at Maddy who is now eating a candy cane.

                    NAT:
          Wait, you're eating a candy cane?

                    MADDY:
          It's refreshing! And sticky.

Maddy has peppermint all around her lips and chin. Her
hands are sticking to everything she touches. Nat looks up
at the ceiling over Maddy's shoulder. We see a camera with
a red light on it, filming their every move. We cut to see
them being recorded on security footage.

                    NAT:
          What's that light up in the corner?

                    MADDY:
          Oh, it looks like a camera.

Maddy puts her fingers in her ears and sticks out her
tongue at the camera. She puts the candy cane around her
neck and pulls herself in and out of frame.

                    MADDY:
          Mmmllawww!

                    NAT:
          Maddy! Somebody's watching us in that camera!

                    MADDY:
          Oh, geez.

Both kids pull their hoods up over their heads and pull
their hats down so the camera cannot recognize them.
We hear a door open down a corridor.

                    NAT:
          (Whispering) We're not alone. Quick…hide!

The kids begin to tiptoe backwards, away from the sound.
We see the Cookie Crook tiptoeing backwards from the other
way. Nat and the Crook bump into each other, butt to butt.

                    NAT:
          Ahhhhh!

                    TOM:
     Ahhhhh!

Nat realizes it's the Cookie Crook from his "dream."

                    NAT:
     You!

                    TOM:
     You!

Maddy sees the Cookie Crook for the first time.

                    MADDY:
     Ewww!

Nat steps back and grabs the now-pointed candy cane from
Maddy. He holds it like a sword.

                    NAT:
     En Guard!

                    TOM:
     Eh. Wait…There's two of you?

                    MADDY:
     Yeah. Turkey Man. We're the Buckleberry twins.
     And, you're stone-cold busted!

                    NAT:
     That's right!

                    TOM:
     Buckleberry? That name sounds familiar.

                    NAT:
     What my sister is trying to say is that we've got
     you! The famous, Christmas Cookie Crook! We found
     you. And now, you're gonna turn yourself in to
     the authorities.

                    TOM:
     For?

                    NAT:
     For stealing all the Christmas cookies in
     Frankincense…and beyond…probably.

                    TOM:
Wait a minute…

                    MADDY:
No, you wait a minute, you cookie-crooking snake
with chicken wings. You've ruined our Christmas.
So, today is your day of reckoning. We've got all
the evidence we need right here in your evil
lair!
                    TOM:
Whoa! This is not *my* evil lair!

                    NAT:
Then what is this? Santa's walk-in closet?

                    TOM:
No-no-no. This place is owned by an old man named
Jahosaphat. The guy hates Christmas. He makes
Ebeneezer Scrooge look like a snow angel. He's
the one who organized the stealing of all this
stuff. He's got a whole army of thieves he uses
to ruin Christmas.

                    NAT:
But, I saw you in my house, stealing cookies.

                    TOM:
I didn't say I didn't steal cookies. But
Jahosaphat forced me to. He gave me a Christmas
serum that took away my Christmas spirit and made
me forget who I really am and where I came from.

                    MADDY:
That's horrible.

                    NAT:
Don't believe a word this freak is saying, Maddy.
He's lying.

                    TOM:
I'm not lying. We've been poisoned by this man to
carry out his plan and ruin Christmas. All this
Christmas stuff is everything we've all stolen
over the years. All part of making everything
Christmas… disappear.

                    MADDY:
So, if you don't know who you are, how do you
know you're not this Jahosaphat's son or
something.

                    TOM:
Well, I don't know if you noticed but, I have
wings.

The Cookie Crook suddenly puffs out his wings. Maddy is
shocked at their unimpressive size. Nat has seen them
before so he's not as taken back.

                    MADDY:
Oh, Ghost of Thurl Ravenscroft, they're grrreat!

                    TOM:
Right?

                    NAT:
Does this Jahosaphat have wings too?

                    TOM:
No. That's how I know I'm not related. Look, I
don't know how I got them. I don't know why I
have them. All I know is I haven't been using
them for good, like the old man said. When I
figured out this serum had such awful affects on
me, I stopped eating it. My head began to feel
clearer. I escaped from my cage and now I'm on
the lamb.

                    MADDY:
What does that mean?

                    TOM:
On the lamb? I think it's a figure of speech…I
think it means I'm on the run.

                    MADDY:
Oh.

                    TOM:
Point is, they're looking for me. And I don't
know how to get away. And they're probably
looking for you now too.

                    NAT:
     Who?

                    TOM:
     Jahosaphat! And the rest of his army of thieves.
     If they find any of us, we're in big trouble.
     And, knowing Jahosaphat, he's got cameras all
     over this facility. Hopefully, you didn't look
     into any of them so they could identify you.

Nat and Maddy look at each other guiltily and knowingly.

                    TOM:
     Tell me you didn't look directly into that camera
     in the corner…

The two kids shrug. Tom reads between the lines.

                    TOM:
     Okay, we've gotta get out of here.

The Cookie Crook and the kids begin to try to find a way
out of the storage facility.
                                             -CUT

INT. IN THE FRONT FOYER OF JAHOSAPHAT'S MANSION -EVENING

Jahosaphat walks angrily through the front door. He begins
to shout out orders. The Humbug Brothers, Azar, Melky,
Gaspar, Edison, Ignacious and others all stand at
attention.
                    JAHOSAPHAT:
     Okay, what have we got, people?

He looks at Edison and the men standing there.

                    AZAR:
     Sir, the most recent camera feed shows the two
     kids are still in the storage facility.

Azar hands Jahosaphat a tablet with a live camera feed on
it. He squints to look at it.

                    JAHOSAPHAT:
Who are they?

                        GEORGE:
Uh, Sir…if I may…

                    JAHOSAPHAT:
Who are you?

                      AZAR:
He's my intern, sir. He's good with tech.

                    JAHOSAPHAT:
Oh…a millennial. Okay, intern, talk.

                        GEORGE:
Sir…our facial recognition equipment identified
the kids as Nat Buckleberry and his sister,
Maddy. They're just two locals from Frankincense.

Jahosaphat swipes through the photos on the tablet and
looks aghast.

                    JAHOSAPHAT:
Oh, no, no, no. This can't be! Those aren't just
two regular kids.

                      AZAR:
Sir, The Cookie Crook is still roaming the halls
of the mansion. He hasn't gotten out yet but I'm
pretty certain he's trying to find a way.

                    JAHOSAPHAT:
Alright, we've got a code red and a code green.
I'm holding you personally responsible for this,
Azar. This would not happen if I had left
Ignacious in charge. Now, how did the Cookie
Crook get out of his cage?

The army of thieves all look at each other, waiting for
each other to speak up. Wondering who will take the
responsibility. Finally, Ignacious steps forward.

IGNACIOUS:
That's uh, that's my fault, sir. I was…I brought
him his dinner and he turned the tables on me.
He's so enchanting.

JAHOSAPHAT:
What? You? C'mon, man. You let him out of his
cage? This is unbelievable! I thought you were
smarter than that, Iggy!

IGNACIOUS:
He told me I was…charming. Said I had,
"character."

JAHOSAPHAT:
Character? You? Ugh! I'll bring you back to
reality after we find these kids and the Cookie
Crook. We need to check every nook and cranny of
this place!

All the army members begin to run around and bump into each
other, trying to figure out which way to go and what to do.

JAHOSAPHAT:
I want all exits sealed and guarded. All cameras
on, all lights on, all hands on deck! If we don't
find these three immediately, our whole plan will
come crashing down. This is a code blue.

IGNACIOUS:
Code Blue?

We see Azar give the signal and blue lights begin to turn
on and an alarm begins to sound.

JAHOSAPHAT:
We've got to make it a Blue Christmas and we
can't do it with these three on the loose!
Edison, take the West wing. Ignacious, take the
roof. Gaspar, Azar, Melky… three wise men like
you should be able to use your gifts to get those
kids in the storage area. Go! Capture them. Bring
them to me. Humbugs, you and I will take the East
wing and work around the perimeter. Go!
Now!...Go!

The thieves all stand there for a moment, until Jahosaphat gives them the order to move, then they scramble out of the foyer and go different directions in the mansion.

                                                            -CUT

INT. THE CAVE ON THE SNOWY HILL -SAME EVENING

The villagers from the search party are cold and shivering, huddled in the cave. They look doomed.

                    CHAZ:
          I don't know how that old man was able to fool
          all of us. I mean, me and the boys've all got our
          college diplomas. Clarence is a
          neuroscientist…Clem's a PhD. We're smart people.

                    POLICE CHIEF:
          We were all duped, Chaz. By a con man. We took
          what he said at face value and it came back to
          bite us.
                    CHAZ:
          Well, he wasn't no bloodhound. More like one of
          them little Shih Tzus. The only thing that could
          save us now is a Christmas miracle.

                    SFX:
          The strange screech of something unusual coming
          from the back of the cave.

Suddenly, deep in the cave, we see eyes glowing. The Villagers stand ready to defend themselves. Then, it gets closer and The Police Chief shines his flashlight on it, revealing that it's a turkey with no wings.

                    SFX:
          Turkey screech.

                    POLICE CHIEF:
          Everyone relax! It's just a turkey.
          A…weird…wingless turkey.

                    COLBY:
          That's a big, wingless turkey.

Colby approaches the turkey and begins to pet the bird.

                    COLBY:
          It's okay, big fella, we're not going to hurt
          you. Settle down, settle down. Now, what happened
          to your wings? Who did this to you?

The turkey turns its head a bit to see all the Villagers.
Then he screeches again and opens his beak. Inside his beak
is a key.

                    COLBY:
          Chief! It's a key! The crazy bird's got a key in
          his mouth.

                    POLICE CHIEF:
          It's a beak. And it's the key to this lock.

The Police Chief grabs the key out of the turkey's beak.
He uses the key to open the door. The chief, deputies and
the villagers all hurry out of the cave. Suddenly, a
snowcat pulls up in front of the cave. The villagers look
frightened—including the Chief. The driver's side window
rolls down. Behind the wheel is Emily in a parka, looking
tough. Inside are all the women from the cookie exchange.
Merry is in the passenger seat.

                    EMILY:
          Get in!

                    MERRY:
          Daddy! Nat and Maddy are missing!

                    POLICE CHIEF:
          What?

                    MERRY:
          We need your help.

The rescue team all pile into the snow cat. The turkey hops
into the vehicle too. The women all drape the rescuers in
blankets.

                    POLICE CHIEF:
          It's a long story.

                    CHAZ:
     I've never been in an Uber before!

                    EMILY:
     Buckle up, pip squeak. We've got some more
     rescuing to do!

She punches the accelerator, shifts the stick shift and the
snow vehicle races down the snowy hill.

                                        -CUT

INT. IN THE STORAGE FACILITY -SAME EVENING

                    TOM:
     We gotta get run outta here…fast.

                    NAT:
     Man. I wish we could fly.

                    MADDY:
     Fly…Yeah, guys...I'm not trying to be too simple
     here but don't you have wings?

The kids and the Crook look at the wings on the his back.

                    TOM:
     I do.

                    MADDY:
     Well, can you literally fly?

                    TOM:
     I'm pretty sure I can.

                    MADDY:
     Well?

There is a slight pause as neither Nat or The Crook seem to
know what Maddy's getting at. Then, it dawns on them both.

                    TOM:
     Oh. Right…I can! Hop aboard and I'll get us out
     of here.

The two kids jump on the Cookie Crook's back and they fly around the huge storage area for a moment. The Cookie Crook picks up speed as if he's going to ram a door down. But, just as he gets close enough, he stops in mid flight and hovers. He reaches into the pocket of his overalls and pulls out a ring with one key on it. He lands and the kids pile off.

                    NAT:
          Wait, you have a key?

                    TOM:
          Skeleton key. Made two of them myself. One went
          missing, but I made 'em both to fit every lock,
          ever. Except the one in my cage. That one was of
          the combination variety.

The Snitcher uses the key to unlock the door and pushes it open.

                    MADDY:
          My daddy was a locksmith.

                    TOM:
          Hm. Interesting coincidence. Jump aboard. We'd
          better get the get.

The kids climb back on and they fly off down the hallway.

                                             -CUT

INT. JAHOSAPHAT'S MANSION -NIGHT.

Jahosaphat is steaming mad and taking it out on the other members of his "army."

                    JAHOSAPHAT:
          Where are those kids! I want them…now!

Azar and George come running into the room.

                    AZAR:
          Sir, we have something that could interest you.

Azar motions to George who opens his laptop so Jahosaphat can see it.

                    JAHOSAPHAT:
        What?

                      AZAR:
        George here matched the kids faces in our data
        base. The machine can connect them to any family
        members within the tri-county area. So, here's
        the kids…

The screen shows the kids photos as a digital line scans
them. Then, their names come up under their photos.

                    JAHOSAPHAT:
        Nat and Maddy Buckleberry, I know that.

                      AZAR:
        And, this is where it gets weird…here's who they
        matched with…

Another digital line connects the kids to another picture.
As it scans, we see the photo is of the Cookie Crook.

                      AZAR:
        They're his kids, sir. The children are the
        Cookie Crook's!

Jahosaphat gets even angrier.

                    JAHOSAPHAT:
        (PAUSE) You fools! I know who they are and I
        don't care who they are…

He knocks the laptop out of George's hands and it smashes
to the ground.

                    JAHOSAPHAT:
        Capture them and put them all in the cage!

                     GEORGE:
        But…that was my personal laptop!

Jahosaphat storms away.

                                              -CUT

INT. -JAHOSAPHAT'S MANSION IN A LONG HALLWAY.

The Cookie Crook glides confidently down the long hallway
with his two new friends on his back.

                         TOM:
          You know, there's something so familiar about you
          two. I just feel like I know you from somewhere.

                         NAT:
          Same.

                         TOM:
          I mean, I'm just getting this weird vibe.
          Like...

                     MADDY & NAT:
          Watch out!

Edison is standing in the hallway, waiting. She reaches her
longs arm up and grabs the Cookie Crook out of mid air and
holds on. He pulls her off the ground as she holds tight.
The kids get jerked on his back but hold on for dear life.
The take a sharp right, trying to shake Edison.

                         TOM:
          Dagnabit!

The kids and the Cookie Crook continue to fly out of
control as Edison holds tight. He is now flying up a large
staircase. He reaches the top and takes a left. Edison's
weight is pulling him down. Tom flies over the heads of the
Humbug Brothers. They chase after him. Up ahead, there's an
open window. Tom makes a break for it. He flies through the
window, there's a balcony below. Something drops out of
Tom's pocket. It's the photo of his wife in the frame. It
hits the ground and shatters.

On the balcony, Melky, Gaspar and Azar hold a giant
butterfly net. They capture the Crook, the kids and Edison.
In super slo-motion, Tom turns inside the net. He wraps his
wings around the kids in mid-air. He barrel rolls as they
all tumble to the ground below and into the snow-protecting
his children. They land right at the feet of Jahosaphat and
the rest of the army. The three wise men look down from the
balcony, then turn and run for the stairs to join their

team. Tom is now on his knees with his wings tucked around
the kids.

                         TOM:
              Gee willikers!

He opens his one wing to see Maddy completely fine. She
smiles at him. He opens the other to see Nat is passed out.
He begins to panic.

                         TOM:
              Oh no…c'mon Squirt. Wake up.

                         MADDY:
              Nat! Wake up!

Tom shakes the little boy.

                         TOM:
              Stay with me, kid!

We see members of the army suddenly looking concerned.
Except Jahosaphat.

                    JAHOSAPHAT:
              (CALMLY/EVILY) Tsk, tsk, tsk…Look what you've
              done, Thomas. You were right when I met you…you
              can't do anything right.

Cut to Maddy looking surprised.

                         MADDY:
              Thomas?

                         TOM:
              Actually…I've done a lot right.

                         MADDY:
              Thomas? Did he just call you Thomas?

Tom, who is on one knee attending to Nat, looks lovingly at
his daughter, both suddenly realizing that they're
connected. Then, he's consumed in helping the little boy.
He waves his wing in front of the kid. In the meantime, all
the army members have gathered around and they seem
concerned about Nat.

                    TOM:
C'mon, kid!

                    JAHOSAPHAT:
You see? This is what Christmas brings…tragedy.
People all stressed out, running all around,
doing this and that. Forgetting about everything
else because they're so tied up in the holidays.
Well, let me tell you…There's no "magic" of
Christmas. It's all something dreamt up by, by
dreamers. December 25th is just the day before
December 26th. Just another day on the calendar.
That's all it should ever be!

Suddenly, Nat comes to.

                    TOM:
That's my boy. Wait…my boy. My girl! My kids! I
remember now! You're my kids. Nat…Maddy! My
wonderful kids!

Tom lifts Nat up from the snow and wraps his wings around
the boy and his sister.
                    TOM:
I'm your father. I'm your dad!

                    NAT:
Dad?

                    MADDY:
I knew it! As soon as you took us under your
wing. I knew it had to be true!

The kids hug their dad. Jahosaphat looks around to see that
his army is beginning to get soft. They all look emotional
seeing the family reimported in front of them.

                    JAHOSAPHAT:
Well, isn't that sweet. The little brats get
their dastardly daddy back. But, you'll come to
your senses and see that moments like this—just
like Christmas. Are just a big waste of time.

Nat hears the words and flashes back to Mr. Griswold, his
counselor saying virtually the same thing. He sudddenly
figures out that Jahosaphat and Mr. Griswold are the same
person.

                    NAT:
Wait…Mr. Griswold? You're Mr. Griswold!

                 JAHOSAPHAT:
Well, look at the pesky little trouble-maker, Nat
Buckleberry, figuring it all out. Realizing that
sometimes adults aren't who we pretend to be!

                    TOM:
He's <u>not</u> who he pretends to be.

                    NAT:
I knew you were no good from the beginning, Mr.
Griswold. That's probably not even your real
name!

                 JAHOSAPHAT:
Oh, ya think?

                    NAT:
I told you about this guy, Maddy. He was the new
counselor at school. He hates Christmas. And he
wants kids to hate it too. Dude's the worst. And
a bad counselor too.

                    TOM:
He's not good people.

                 JAHOSAPHAT:
So naïve. Like father, like son. A family of
fools! I am Jahosaphat Higgins the 3rd. I'm a rich
man and a scoundrel. A master of disguise and a
manipulator of the weak and vulnerable! And I am
the official, original hater of all things
Christmas!

                   MADDY:
This guy's off his rocker.

                 JAHOSAPHAT:
The way I see it, I've just added two new members
to my army. The Buckleberry twins. Two little
scoundrels. I'll put both of you little brats to
work, in charge of stealing packages off people's
porches and replacing them with coal.

MADDY:
That's not very original.

JAHOSAPHAT:
I'll call you The Coal Kids. That's it! Nat and
Natalie Coal. Er… Something.

MADDY:
That's definitely not original.

JAHOSAPHAT:
Oh, you'll be despicable! All of you…it's time to
get back to work. We've got Christmas to ruin!
I'll…

Suddenly, the Snow Cat appears. Jahosaphat tries to run out
of the way but gets covered with snow. The top of the
vehicle opens and the ladies hose him down with water. He
freezes immediately. Tom, Nat and Maddy watch in disbelief
as The Police Chief, Merry and the rest of the rescue team
pile out of the vehicle. Merry runs right toward the kids.
Tom has his back to her.

MERRY:
Maddy! Nat!

Tom stands up to face his wife for the first time in years.

MERRY:
Thomas? Is it really you?

TOM:
I think so.

NAT:
I found him, Mom! I told you I would!

MADDY:
We found him!

People in the crowd begin to tear up as we watch the
reunion unfold. Thomas throws his wings around his wife and
kids.
KATHERINE:
Now that truly warms the cockles of your heart.

Melky tries to put his arm around Katherine.

MELKY:
Permission to put a friendly, comforting arm
around you?

KATHERINE:
Touch me and I'll introduce you to Fi-Fi.

Fi-fi—in Katherine's purse—growls at Melky.

MELKY:
Not necessary. Good doggie.

Jahosaphat looks like an ice Christmas tree. His tongue
pushes through the ice, allowing him to talk.

JAHOSAPHAT:
Wait a minute! Edison, Azar, Melky, Gaspar…
guys…seize all of these people! Make them pay for
what they've done to me!

The army members look mystified. Edison walks over to the
ice tree (Jahosaphat). She reaches into her pocket.

JAHOSAPHAT:
That's my girl.

She takes a light bulb out of her pocket, licks the bottom
of it, puts it at the top of the ice tree and rotates it.
It lights up.

JAHOSAPHAT:
Oh, no you didn't...

The Police Chief takes out his handcuffs and realizes they
won't work on frozen Jahosaphat.

POLICE CHIEF:
Uh…Jahosaphat B. Higgins The Third? You're under
arrest for extortion, thievery, lying, cheating,
kidnapping…I'm basically throwing the book at
you. And you're going away to chill out for a
long, long time.

JAHOSAPHAT:
I'm already chilling!

                    POLICE CHIEF:
Load him up, boys.

                    JAHOSAPHAT:
No! Wait a minute! I want my lawyer! I had
nothing to do with this! These people did it! I
didn't do anything wrong!

Deputies and Chaz push Jahosaphat over, then load him on
top of the Snow Cat like a real Christmas tree. The Police
Chief approaches Tom, Merry and the kids. A deputy stops
him.

                    COLBY:
Chief! I'm pretty sure this is the group who've
been stealing all the Christmas stuff.

                    POLICE CHIEF:
What?

                    COLBY:
We found tons of candy canes, millions of gallons
of egg nog, Christmas light bulbs, gingerbread…

                    DEPUTY 2:
Don't forget the mistletoe!

                    COLBY:
Oh…yep…mistletoe. Everything's stored in the
basement of this place. We even found the source
of the fruitcakes that are being delivered all
over town. Some sicko, this guy was, passing out
fruitcakes. These weirdos did it all!

                    TOM:
Whoa, whoa, whoa…Wait a minute! These people
aren't weirdos. They're victims, just like us.
Jahosaphat turned all of them into thieves. He
put anti-Christmas serum in their food and
trained them to carry out his evil plan. They're
just regular people forced to do terrible things.
Like me. They don't need punishment. They need
rehabilitation. They need love.

We pan Jashosaphat's Army who all look forlorn and
remorseful. Chaz and Clem appear.

                    CHAZ:
The turkey-man is on to something, Chief. We just
found this in the old man's lab.

Clem is holding a gallon container marked, "Anti-Christmas
Serum."

                 POLICE CHIEF:
Anti-Christmas Serum? Leave them alone, Deputy.
They've been through a lot...We all have.

                    COLBY:
But…

                 POLICE CHIEF:
Ah!

The Chief puts a hand up to silent Deputy Colby. Then, he
turns his attention to Tom, Merry and the kids.

                 POLICE CHIEF:
Tom…I…I didn't like when you married Merry
because you were taking my daughter from me. But,
I gotta be honest, I don't feel the same anymore.
I actually like that you had your quirks. It made
you who you were. Now, I don't know much about
sharing my feelings. And I may not know how to be
a good father…

The Chief looks at Merry. Then, at his grandkids, then his
wife, then back at Tom.

                 POLICE CHIEF:
Or, a good grandfather…or, ah… the best husband,
for that matter. But, I do know that a man
doesn't need wings to fly. He just needs an
adjustment. Merry and the kids have been
miserable without you. They've missed you, Tom.
And I've…I've missed you too…son.

                    TOM:
Son?

The Police Chief can only nod his head, he's choked up.

                    TOM:
Bring it in here, you old lug!

Tom extends his wings and the Chief joins the hug.

                    POLICE CHIEF:
          This is…I've been needing this.

                         TOM:
          Group hug, everyone!

Everybody comes in for an awkward hug. Tom looks over at
the wingless turkey and invites him into the group hug.
The turkey obliges and is embraced by Chaz, Ellenore and
Maddy. He reaches in. George appears.

                       GEORGE:
          Mr. Buckleberry, I found this. I think it's
          yours.

George hands Tom the photo of his family from the frame.

                         TOM:
          Aw. Gee willikers. Thanks!

Tom pulls the photo out of the broken frame, then,
continues the hug. George joins the hug.

                       GEORGE:
          He broke my laptop too.

Nat's pressed against an adult and can barely talk.

                         NAT:
          Dad…Dad…it's December 24th.

                         TOM:
          I know, son.

                         NAT:
          That means we only have a couple of hours.

It suddenly dawns on Tom that he's got something to do.

                         TOM:
          A couple hours for what?

                    NAT:
     A couple hours to bring Christmas back to
     Frankincense.

                    TOM:
     Geez-o-Pete, Squirt, you're right. We've got some
     work to do. Everyone, lend a hand! We've got some
     Christmas spirit to deliver!

The people in the hug begin to move as a whole, not
breaking the hug.

                    TOM:
     Okay, we're going to have to break up this hug.
     Okay, on the count of three…one…two…and break.

They all finally pull apart from each other and begin to
scurry.

                    TOM:
     Come with me, everyone! To the storage room!

                                                  -CUT

EXT. MORNING—ALL OVER FRANKINCENSE.

                    VILLAGERS:

     (SINGING)
     It's egg nog to sip on and slippers to slip on
     It's being with friends and candy to share.
     It's beautiful lighting and a house so inviting
     A brisk walk outside and a warm teddy bear.
     It's the little things that truly make up
     Christmas
     The tiny things, like cocoa when it's hot
     The little things put meaning into Christmas.
     And Christmas Cookies truly mean a lot.

A montage that includes scenes of the Snow Cat with
Katherine and Chaz in it, while The Egg Nog Napper delivers
bottles of egg nog to every doorstep and deputies hand out
candy canes all over town with Azar. Edison replaces bulbs
on strings of lights while The Police Chief stands nearby.
Gaspar, Merry and the other women put gingerbread houses in
storefronts in downtown Frankincense. A shadow passes
overhead as excited families run outside with their trays
and plates for cookies. For overhead is the Christmas

Cookie Crook, with Nat and Maddy on his back,dropping
parachutes filled with Christmas cookies all over town.

-CUT

EXT. AND INT.—CHRISTMAS DAY, IN THE BUCKLEBERRY HOUSE

NARRATOR:

The magic of Christmas in my expertise
Is not the treats, or the cookies or, the lights
on the trees. What makes it so special—If you
took all that away, Is that friends and family
Come first on that day.

Nat, Maddy, Merry and Tom,David and Margaret are sitting
around, opening presents. Tom still has bandages around his
shoulders where doctors removed his wings. The turkey walks
into the room. His wings have been reattached and bandaged
too. Maddy gives the turkey a hug as if he's the family
dog. Merry sits next to Tom on the couch, excited about the
present he's about to open. It's a new frame. Tom knows
what to do. He reaches into his bathrobe pocket and pulls
out the photo of his wife and kids. He slides it into the
new frame. He shows the rest of the family. The two kids
hug their mom and dad.

www.ingramcontent.com/pod-product-compliance
Lightning Source LLC
Chambersburg PA
CBHW061306120726
48001CB00001B/497